The Rhythm Method

Also From Kylie Scott

Pause
Fake
The Rich Boy
Lies
Repeat
It Seemed Like a Good Idea at the Time
Trust

THE DIVE BAR SERIES
Dirty
Twist
Chaser

THE STAGE DIVE SERIES
Lick
Play
Lead
Deep
Strong: A Stage Dive Novella
Love Song
The Rhythm Method

THE FLESH SERIES
Flesh
Skin
Flesh Series Novellas

Heart's a Mess
Colonist's Wife

The Rhythm Method
A Stage Dive Novella
By Kylie Scott

1001 DARK NIGHTS
PRESS

The Rhythm Method
A Stage Dive Novella
By Kylie Scott

Copyright 2021 Kylie Scott
ISBN: 978-1-951812-76-8

Published by 1001 Dark Nights Press, an imprint of Evil Eye
Concepts, Incorporated

Sign up for the 1001 Dark Nights Newsletter
and be entered to win a Tiffany Key necklace.

There's a contest every month!

Go to www.1001DarkNights.com to subscribe.

**As a bonus, all subscribers can download
FIVE FREE exclusive books!**

One Thousand and One Dark Nights

Once upon a time, in the future…

*I was a student fascinated with stories and learning.
I studied philosophy, poetry, history, the occult, and
the art and science of love and magic. I had a vast
library at my father's home and collected thousands
of volumes of fantastic tales.*

*I learned all about ancient races and bygone
times. About myths and legends and dreams of all
people through the millennium. And the more I read
the stronger my imagination grew until I discovered
that I was able to travel into the stories… to actually
become part of them.*

*I wish I could say that I listened to my teacher
and respected my gift, as I ought to have. If I had, I
would not be telling you this tale now.
But I was foolhardy and confused, showing off
with bravery.*

*One afternoon, curious about the myth of the
Arabian Nights, I traveled back to ancient Persia to
see for myself if it was true that every day Shahryar
(Persian: شهريار, "king") married a new virgin, and then
sent yesterday's wife to be beheaded. It was written
and I had read that by the time he met Scheherazade,
the vizier's daughter, he'd killed one thousand
women.*

Something went wrong with my efforts. I arrived in the midst of the story and somehow exchanged places with Scheherazade – a phenomena that had never occurred before and that still to this day, I cannot explain.

Now I am trapped in that ancient past. I have taken on Scheherazade's life and the only way I can protect myself and stay alive is to do what she did to protect herself and stay alive.

Every night the King calls for me and listens as I spin tales. And when the evening ends and dawn breaks, I stop at a point that leaves him breathless and yearning for more. And so the King spares my life for one more day, so that he might hear the rest of my dark tale.

As soon as I finish a story... I begin a new one... like the one that you, dear reader, have before you now.

Prologue

Chandeliers twinkled overhead, and a string quartet played *Led Zeppelin*. All while our friends and family ate and drank and made merry. Out the nearest window you could see the Eiffel Tower all lit up for the night, and I couldn't have been happier if I tried. The hotel suite was wonderful. Everything was perfect. Just perfect.

"Here you go," said my husband, David, passing me a Moscow mule. "Happy seventh wedding anniversary, Mrs. Ferris."

"Right back at you, Mr. Ferris."

He pressed a kiss to my lips. "Who the hell would have thought?"

"We had a rough start." I smiled. "But I sure am glad we persevered."

"Me too. This dress you're wearing…" His fingers traced down my spine in a thrilling fashion. My back was bared by the low square cut of the short, black Hervé Legér fit and flare dress. It also had a plunging v-neckline, and my man definitely noticed. "Have I said how much I appreciate the easy access?"

"I may have learned a thing or two about how you like it," I said coyly.

"We are in the city of love."

"Hmm."

"It's not like we'd be missed." He nuzzled the side of my neck, making my toes curl. "What do you say, baby?"

"You want us to sneak out of our own party?"

"It wouldn't be the first time."

I nodded. "True."

"Did I mention we're in the city of love?" he asked, nibbling on my earlobe.

"Yes. I believe you did."

We were in France because Stage Dive was doing a world tour. It started three months ago and would continue on for another ten. A whole year and a bit on the road with one of the biggest rock bands in the world. From North America to Europe, Asia, Australia, New Zealand, South America, and then back home again. Not all of the family would be on the whole tour. People had lives and children had school and so on.

But tonight they were all here. Just for this. For us. And the celebration of our seven years together. I'd intended it to be a casual get-together, but this was so much better. Everyone dressed up to the nines and was having the time of their life. Touring was hard work with constant stresses, and we deserved some fun.

"Coming through," hollered Mal, the blond drummer.

David and I separated to allow the dance line to pass. Because even fancy parties in France needed a dance line, apparently. First came Mal bopping along with his two-year-old son, Tommy, on his shoulders. Followed by five-year-old Gibson and his dad, Ben, the tall, bearded bassist. Behind them came the band's lead singer, Jimmy, with his twin girls. They were almost six and would in all likelihood be taking over the planet any day now. Hooray for strong women. Their father couldn't have been any more delighted with their energy and enthusiasm for life. Jimmy might have been the slick bad boy of the band back in the day, but he'd grown into a good man and a great father.

At the very end of the line was Sam, our head of security. Clad in his usual black suit with a poker face few could match, he nodded briefly as he danced past. "Excuse us, Mrs. Ferris." As hard as I tried, I couldn't get him to call me by my first name.

"Not a problem, Sam."

"Lovely night."

I grinned, saluting them with my drink. "It sure is."

When Tommy noisily demanded to be put down, his father complied. The small child immediately ran past the buffet, swiping several macaroons, before disappearing behind the chaise. This excellent idea was seized upon by all three of the other children, and soon enough, the macaroon tray sat empty and the kids grew increasingly hyper.

"They're going to be on a sugar high for days," said David, cozying up to me again.

"Lena's flying home with the girls tomorrow. Can you imagine all that energy in a confined space?"

He grunted. "Terrifying."

"That'll be us one day."

"In about five years," he agreed, taking a swig from his bottle of beer. Because you could take the rock star to Paris and dress him in a three-piece suit, but he still wouldn't be sipping champagne. Thank you very much.

"That's the plan," I said.

"And you do like your plans."

The man was right about that. Some people could go through life flying by the seat of their pants. Content to not know what would happen next. I was not one of those people. I both knew and accepted this about myself. Know thyself and all that. Lists were my friends. Neatly ordered inventories of anything and everything going on in my life. Places to be. Things to do. Targets to be achieved at work. Planning was how I gave shape and context to my existence which in turn helped me live life to the fullest. Not that I didn't mind taking a walk on the wild side now and then. I had woken up in Vegas married to a rock star, after all. But being organized was where I thrived. It was my happy place.

"I say we enjoy ourselves while we can." His fingers crept beneath my long blonde hair to rub my neck. Guitarists' hands were wonderful things. So much strength and dexterity. Not to mention the creativity.

I raised a brow. "Are you talking about the bathroom again?"

"The way I figure it, this suite has four rooms," he said, voice low and husky. Sexy as fuck. My panties grew damper with every word he whispered. "The bedroom, bathroom, dining room, and this formal parlor or whatever the hell the butler called it. Now, given how much we're paying per night, it would be wrong of us to not make the most of the place."

"Oh."

"Four rooms is well within our abilities."

"I'd hope so. I only turned twenty-eight yesterday."

"Exactly," he said as Led Zeppelin changed to The Rolling Stones. "And we just renewed our membership in the mile high club yesterday for your birthday."

I gave him a distinctly cat-got-the-cream sort of smile.

"Now here we are. It's the city of love, baby. So let's go make it."

"Oh my God." I laughed. "You better play exceptionally well here, because you're getting so much mileage out of this city of love thing."

My husband nipped me on the neck, making me jump. Just a little.

"No biting," announced a small voice. "Don't, Uncle Davie."

"Shit. Tommy." David swallowed. "Didn't see you there, buddy."

The child with the mop of wild blond hair stared up at us with a horrified expression. "You sweared!"

"Busted," I muttered.

Tommy lifted his arms in a silent demand to be picked up, and David did as asked. Once the boy was settled on my husband's hip, he pursed his lips, thinking deep thoughts. "Want cookies."

David bit back a smile. "Do you now?"

Tommy just blinked, the picture of innocence.

"We're all out of cookies, sorry," I answered. "How about an apple?"

"No."

"Some berries?"

The small child screwed his nose up in disgust. "No-o-o."

"No to apples and berries, huh? Well, what about a nice yummy turnip?"

"Yuck."

I tapped a finger against my chin in contemplation. "What would you say to a lovely big cabbage, then?"

He shook his small head fiercely, and David cracked a smile.

"Broccoli? Asparagus? Onion?"

Tommy giggled. "No, Aunty Ev. No!"

"Are you threatening my child with vegetables again?" Mal tickled his son, making him wriggle like a worm. "That's just sick and wrong. How could you, Child Bride?"

"Chide bwide," repeated Tommy dutifully.

"How long are you going to continue with that?" I took a sip of my drink. "I'm heading toward thirty, for heaven's sake."

Mal just winked.

David had no sooner handed the boy over than Tommy squirmed to be set down. Little legs pumping, he was off and running. Mal shook his head. "They never stop. And that's why he will be an only child."

"Yeah?" asked David.

Mal shook his head. "Oh, yeah. Phew. One and done."

Pale arms wrapped around Mal's middle as his redheaded wife Anne joined the conversation. "I didn't know you felt that way."

"But we discussed this," said Mal. "I know we did."

"Was this like the time we discussed turning one of the bedrooms into a giant ball pit? Or was I actually awake when this conversation happened?"

He shrugged. "Maybe not, now that you mention it. Tommy was around six months old, and he had one of those diaper explosions where it went right up the back. Never been so traumatized in all my life."

"I thought one more might be nice." Anne rested her head against his arm. "Maybe you could think about it."

"We do make pretty babies."

"This is true."

"And you get incredibly horny when you're pregnant. Once you stop puking, that is."

"That's not my fault," said Anne. "There's a lot of hormones going on. They stir things up in me, in both cases."

Mal grinned. "Then the tit fairy visits. I love it when that happens. They get so sensitive."

Anne looked to heaven, but there was no help forthcoming.

"But enough about you," said Mal. "Really, the world deserves, nay needs, more of my DNA. Think of it, a legion of ridiculously good looking drumming artistes."

David snorted.

"Shut up, Davie," griped Mal. "Petty jealousy is beneath you, bro."

"Hold on. A legion?" Anne's brows rose. "I was just thinking of a sibling for Tommy."

"Only one? How could you be so selfish, Pumpkin?"

A little line appeared between Anne's brows as she stared at her husband in wonder or maybe bewilderment. Possibly both.

"If we had three then they could start a band and be like Hansen or the Jonas Brothers."

"Oh, that's definitely worth considering," I added. Because encouraging the lunatic drummer sometimes was just an honor and a privilege.

"Thought they were all going to be drummers?" David tucked a strand of long hair behind his ear. "How's that going to work?"

"Awesomely," said Mal.

Anne held back laughter.

"No, Tommy. Please don't put that up your nose. Thank you, son. I appreciate your restraint." Mal gave his wife a look. "Definitely gets that from your side of the family, Pumpkin."

"While it's been great to share all of this deeply personal information with our nearest and dearest," said Anne, "why don't we revisit this topic once the tour is over and we've had a chance to catch our breath?"

Mal pressed a kiss to her lips.

Just then, the string quartet started playing *Jackson* by Johnny Cash and June Carter Cash. One of my all-time favorite songs and kind of relevant to how we'd started. Because we sure had gotten married in a fever. A drunken one. Next a stupendous croquembouche decorated with bright fresh flowers and golden lines of delicate spun sugar was wheeled in with much pomp and pageantry. Everyone started clapping.

"Cake," yelled Tommy.

"Wow. Who did this?" I asked, my face hurting from smiling so hard.

Jimmy sketched me a bow from across the room, and I blew him a kiss. Best brother-in-law ever.

David slipped his hands beneath my hair, placing a white gold diamond solitaire pendant around my neck. "Happy anniversary, baby."

"Oh my, God. It's beautiful." I wound my arms around his neck and held on tight. "Thank you."

He pressed a kiss to my forehead. "I love you."

"I love you too," I said, getting teary. "Everything is absolutely perfect."

He gave me a devil may care grin. "And it's going to stay that way."

Chapter One

Everything was about as far from perfect as it could get. Life-altering things have a habit of happening to me on bathroom floors. Approximately seven years and eight and a bit months ago I woke up in Vegas hungover and married to a rock star. Now this was happening...

"Oh, fuck!"

Another tight and terrible cramp seized me around the middle. I gritted my teeth and panted and just generally did my best to live through it. Damn, it hurt. And they were coming closer together now. Somehow I was going to have to get to my feet and reach the cell I'd left on the bed. I'd put off calling an ambulance, but this was ridiculous. Obviously something was very wrong. The pain eased, though the general tightness didn't. But at least I could catch my breath.

Why the hell did this have to happen now, today of all days? I was looking forward to joining David for the last few cities of the tour. Stage Dive had been at it for almost a year, circling the globe. I'd been with them off and on, trying to juggle managing my coffee shop in Portland, Oregon, and spending time with my man.

Music streaming services paying next to nothing meant bands needed to tour more now than ever. It wasn't an easy lifestyle to maintain. However, it was almost time for them to come home. I planned to hang out with my husband for the last few shows, then we'd come back together. Which made it the worst damn time for something to go wrong with my insides.

"Child Bride?" The concerned and somewhat surprised voice came from the general vicinity of the living room. "Where are you?"

"Mal? I'm in the bathroom off the main bedroom."

Heavy footsteps rushed up the hallway toward me as I wiped the sweat off my face and wrapped my robe a little tighter. I thought a hot shower would help, and it had for a while. I stood in there with the spray on my back. Now, however, everything sucked to the extreme.

The drummer stuck his blond head around the doorway, and his eyes went wide. "What's wrong?"

"I don't know." And I was done. Guess it was the knowledge I was no longer alone. I burst into tears. "I-I think it's a kidney stone, maybe. Or just really bad period cramps."

"Shit."

"Call an ambulance."

"Yes. Right. On it," he said, pulling his cell out of one of the pockets in his battered black leather jacket. "Yes, hello, my friend is in real bad pain. She thinks it's a kidney stone or period cramps." He listened for a moment before putting his cell on speaker, turning to me. "She's in her late twenties. Ev, describe the pain. When did it start and stuff like that?"

"Um. I had this weird back pain all day while I was working at the café. Then I came home to pack and it just got worse and worse." I stopped to suck in a deep breath, staring up at the ceiling, trying to hold myself together. "I keep needing to sit on the toilet. Like I want to push something out, but nothing's coming out. And the cramps or whatever they keep coming in like waves, closer and closer together. They're really bad."

"Ma'am," said the voice over the cell. "How far apart are the cramps?"

"Every minute or so now." Which was when another ripped through me. "God...fuck!"

"Pre-existing conditions?"

Unable to speak, I shook my head.

"She says no," added Mal.

"An ambulance is on the way," said the voice.

"Thanks." Mal hung up and tossed the cell aside while I cried some more, clutching at my middle. The usually cool and comedic drummer's eyes were wide and panicked. "What can I do to help?"

I opened my mouth wide and yelled. Nothing else would do. My body was tearing itself in two. Slowly, gradually, the pain eased again, and I could think straight for a minute. "Thank God you're here. Why are you here, by the way?"

"Had to come to town for a last minute solo promo thing last night. Plus Anne wanted me to check out a kindergarten she likes for Tommy. Figured I'd catch the jet back to Nashville with you in time for the concert tomorrow. Nothing like catching a red eye across the country."

"Oh."

"You weren't answering your cell, but the doorman said you were in. Thought you must have been asleep," he explained. "I was going to wake you, make sure you didn't miss the flight."

I nodded tiredly.

"I better call Dave."

"No," I panted. "Wait until we know what's wrong. I don't want him to worry. Hopefully the paramedics can give me something, then everything will be fine. Maybe we can still make the concert."

He gave me a look of much disbelief.

"Sorry about the TMI."

"Like that matters." He snorted. "My bedside manner is excellent. I could have been a doctor."

"You could not have been a doctor."

"A great doctor," he continued, ignoring me. "And a brilliant surgeon."

"Dave says you can barely manage holding two sticks at the same time."

"A genius one, really. Probably would have cured everything by now."

"Stop," I said with a weary smile. "Don't make me laugh, I don't have the energy."

"Sorry."

The pain struck me again, and I screamed bloody murder. Mal nearly fell over backwards. It would have been funny if I weren't possibly dying.

Suddenly, my body wanted to push, and I just gave in and did as directed. Nothing in my life had ever felt like this. It was excruciating.

But the weird and awesome thing was something shifted inside me. We were maybe getting somewhere, and oh thank fuck for that. I yelled and pushed and strained with my toes curled and every muscle in my legs and lower abdomen putting in effort. The pain slowly eased again. Just a little. But it kind of felt like it was always there lurking low, near the base of my spine.

"Breathe," ordered Mal, his face tense.

I nodded and panted some more. At least I wasn't alone anymore. Alone had been scary.

"Is this normal for a kidney stone?" he asked.

"No idea."

Then he grabbed a white towel off the wall and stuffed it below my lower body. "The bath mat's wet."

Whatever.

He leaned to the side. "Shit. Ev, the liquid looks all reddish and pink. Think I better have a look and see if you're bleeding."

"Okay."

"Neither of us want this, but…"

"Just do it."

He gently pushed my knees wide apart and froze. "Ah, Ev?"

"What?" I asked as the pain amped up once again. "Oh, motherfucker."

"You might want to push."

"No shit, Mal!"

"Because I think you're sort of having a baby," he finished.

"What? That's ridicu... Argh." I gritted my teeth and ignored his bullshit crazy words and pushed. It was the only thing my body wanted to do. Agony tore through me. If I could just get it out. Whatever it was. Everything would be fine.

He tore another towel off the wall and held it down near my groin. "Keep going. That's it. You're doing great. I can definitely see a head."

Maybe Mal was drunk and delusional. I didn't know. Maybe he was on drugs. But I definitely wasn't pregnant because that wasn't the kind of thing you tended not to notice. Having a baby was sort of a damn big deal. At any rate, I had other things to worry about. Like not dying anytime soon.

Again and again, I pushed for all I was worth. Sweat coated my body, and every inch of me was on fire. It felt like my insides were trying to burst out of me. Gross, but true. Nothing mattered apart from making it happen. Getting whatever it was out.

"Come on, little baby," he said, staring determinedly at my crotch. "That's it. You're doing really well."

The pain dimmed again, giving me room to think. And my thoughts were not happy. "No. Wait. A baby? You're being serious? Like really?"

He grinned. "Yep. Isn't that wild?"

"But...I can't be."

"Yeah, but you sort of are."

"A baby isn't part of the plan. Not for another four or so years." Tears leaked down my face. "No. You're just being silly or something. I think I'd know if I was pregnant, Mal."

He winced. "Ev..."

"I mean, come on! How is that even possible?"

"Not sure we have time for me to explain the birds and the bees to you."

"I'm on birth control," I continued in a calm if somewhat shrieking tone of voice. "My periods are light and irregular, but they're there."

Mal just shrugged. "I honestly don't know what to tell you. Want me to take a picture and show you so you can see for yourself?"

"Don't you dare take a picture of my vagina!"

"Right. Sorry. Bad idea," he said. "Please don't scream at me. The acoustics in this room are intense."

"Oh my God. I'm having a baby, and David isn't even here." My head spun in the weirdest way, but I couldn't faint. It was time to push again. "Ohhh!"

"That's it," said Mal, all excited. "Almost there."

I pushed again, and something roughly the size of Texas slipped out of my nether regions and into Mal's waiting hands. A cranky little cry filled the room, echoing off the tiled walls and floor. The most unexpected and amazing sound I'd ever heard. My head felt light, though, my body felt heavy. How the hell could this be happening?

"It's a boy," said Mal, voice ecstatic.

"A boy? Is he okay?"

"I think so."

He wrapped the baby, my baby, in a clean towel and carefully handed him to me. The smallest, most surprising of things lay on my chest. A tiny perfect nose and rosebud lips. A tuft of dark hair coated in muck clung to his little head. I kept blinking back tears, trying to clear my fuzzy, freaked-out head, but the view never changed. A baby.

"I've got to find scissors and string and stuff," said Mal. "That's what they do on TV."

"The paramedics should be here soon."

"Might be better to wait for the professionals." He sighed. "Holy shit. Talk about adrenaline. My heart is racing. Can't believe I delivered a baby on your bathroom floor."

"You're telling me." I traced a gentle finger over the small one's cheek. Stunned was a great word. It summed up a whole hell of a lot with regards to this situation. "Where the heck did you come from? I don't understand any of this."

"Well, Child Bride, I can say with some authority that he did in fact come out of your lady parts." His smile turned gentle. "You really didn't know you were pregnant?"

Another tear fell down my face. "I didn't have a clue. How did I not know, Mal? What am I going to tell David?"

Loud banging came from the front door.

Mal frowned. "I better get that. Stop freaking out. And give him boob. Babies love boob."

I nodded, transfixed once more by the child's tiny perfect features. My child. Mine and David's. I didn't know if I should cry some more, laugh in a hysterical fashion, or pass out cold. A mixture of all three might be nice. Instead, I just said, "Oh my God."

* * * *

David rushed into the private hospital suite just before six the next morning. His long dark hair was tied back in a ponytail, his long-sleeve tee and black jeans rumpled as if he'd been in them for a day or two. And I, of course, burst into tears at the sight of his face. Because this was what I'd been holding out for. To finally have him here with me so I didn't have to face this alone. But also, my hormones were running wild.

"Baby," he said, rushing over to my bedside. His strong arms closed around me, and for the first time since this all started, I could actually breathe—but guilt still weighed heavily on me.

"I'm a terrible person," I wailed. "A horrible mother. They shouldn't even let me be a parent."

"Bullshit."

"It's true. I drank coffee. I even had a glass of wine last weekend!"

"And the pediatrician said your baby was a little early, but fine." Mal rocked said baby over by the window. He gave David a tired smile. "Hey, man. Want to meet your son?"

"My son." David shook his head. "Fuck. This is…"

"Wonderful," finished Jimmy Ferris, taking a peek at the little burrito sitting in Mal's arms. His smile was wide. "Absolutely fucking wonderful. Congratulations."

David nodded, settling on the mattress beside me. Necessary because I had a death grip on him and wasn't letting go. The last twelve hours may have traumatized me. He smoothed my messy hair and held me tight, letting me get it all out. The fear and the pain and everything. I cried until I was empty, and he held on to me the whole time. Whispering things like, "I'm here. It's okay now. You did great. We're going to be just fine. I love you."

"We weren't even going to start trying to get pregnant for another four years," I said then sobbed my heart out again.

"Hey, baby, listen to me," he said, voice firm. "I know this isn't what we planned. But we're going to be okay."

Finally, I hiccupped and wiped my face. "Can I have a Kleenex?"

David passed me the box, and I blew my nose with nil decorum. Then I had a drink of water. Then I started pulling myself together, piece by piece. We could do this. We would do this. Together. I'd never been so overwhelmed in my life. But everything would be okay.

With a small smile, Mal brought over our unnamed child. "Look how chill he is. He knows he's loved and getting looked after. Everything is cool with him. He's fast asleep and dreaming of milk."

"He's so small," said David, his eyes wide as twin moons.

"Just under seven pounds. A perfectly normal healthy birthweight." Mal carefully handed him over. "Your boy is all good."

On account of the four existing second-generation members of Stage Dive, we all knew how to hold babies. Which was lucky.

David stared, entranced by the baby's face. The man was definitely paler than normal and had dark circles beneath his eyes. His brows sat high, and he kept shaking his head, like he couldn't believe any of this was real. Join the club.

"They think that due to the placement of the placenta, I didn't feel a lot of his movement. And because my uterus is tilted, I didn't carry him out front so much," I said. "I also didn't get any morning sickness, which can happen. I was on contraception, so I never imagined that the breast sensitivity was anything more than hormones acting up. But no birth control is one hundred percent effective, as we've now seen."

"If you're not expecting to get pregnant then you're not going to be looking out for the signs," said Jimmy with a gentle smile. "I think you're incredible, delivering your baby at home like you did."

Mal cleared his throat. "That was mostly me. Doing the incredible stuff...you know. Not to make a big deal out of it or anything."

"I mean, I went up a size a few months back. But I never imagined it was because I had a baby on board." I sighed. "We're so unprepared for this. I don't even know where to begin. It's all so huge."

"Ben and the girls have you covered," said Jimmy. "Lena was taking all the kids to our place while Anne, Lizzy, and he start rounding up everything you'll need. That's why they're not here now."

"Everyone turning up at once would have set off the paps," said David, carefully cradling the baby's head.

"Damn photographers." My shoulders sank in relief. "Oh, thank God about the things for the baby. That's so kind of them to help out."

"We're family, Ev. It's our pleasure." Jimmy winked. "They said if there's anything in particular you want ASAP to give them a call. They're going to set up one of your spare rooms as a nursery. So you should text them if you have any particular colors in mind and care what room they use."

"Right." I tried to smile. But after only a couple hours of sleep, exhaustion owned me.

"Or you can worry about all of that further down the line and just let them handle it for now. Whatever you want."

I nodded. "The second idea sounds seriously good."

"Then let them have at it," said Jimmy. "They spent half of the flight back debating the merit of llamas versus sloths for the nursery décor. Helping you out is not a hardship."

I would not get teary again. I wouldn't. But it was so nice to have our family together again in Portland.

Meanwhile, David stared in wonder at the tiny hand wrapped around one of his much larger fingers. "He's really ours."

"He really is."

"We haven't discussed baby names. Not seriously."

My jaw cracked on a yawn. "No. We haven't."

"Mal Junior is still available. Just throwing that out there," said Mal. "No need to decide right now. Try it out for a few years. See how it feels."

"We'll get right on that," said David, carefully handing the baby over to Jimmy. The baby let out a cry of displeasure. But as the father of twins, he was skilled at soothing babies back to sleep. David rose and approached the drummer. "Thank you, man. You were there for them. Helped Ev through it all. I won't forget it."

Mal shrugged. "Geez. Don't make a big deal out of it, dude. You're embarrassing me. Now that you're here, I'm going to head home and get some sleep. Be back later, okay?"

The two men hugged with lots of back slapping. It was a beautiful thing. Then Mal came over and pressed a gentle kiss to my forehead.

"Thank you for everything, Mal," I said.

"Anytime, Child Bride."

"My son." David stood beside my bed with the baby in his arms. His hands were curled around the precious bundle with the utmost of care. "This is...I still can't get my head around it."

"It's big," I agreed.

"Yet he's so damn little."

I gave him an unsteady smile. "Everything's going to change now."

David's eyes were wide and every now and then he'd sigh. Like he was once again settling into our new reality. Then an amazed sort of smile would tug at his lips as he stared at his son in wonder. "Have you ever seen anything so tiny and perfect?"

"No. Never."

"It's like I want to protect him from everything forever," said David.

"Yeah."

The baby waved his little arms and let out a cry.

"Feeding time?" asked David.

"Probably. He just had a diaper change, so…" I got myself into a comfortable position then held out my arms. David carefully passed the baby to me. "I never gave much thought to breastfeeding, but I kind of like it. Just having quiet time to hang out and be with him, you know?"

David sat on the edge of the mattress to watch. Then he leaned in and lifted the end of the baby's blanket. It had come loose with all of the passing back and forth. With a gentle hand, David counted his toes. "So soft and small."

"He needs a name."

David raised his brows. "A name? Right."

"What've you got?" I smiled. "It's not easy. I've been trying to think of something all night and came up with zip."

"Ah, okay…they were actually throwing ideas around on the plane. I was listening some of the time when I wasn't quietly freaking out and worrying about you." He shrugged. "How about Nash? Short for Nashville and your love of all things country music."

"Good one." I studied the baby's tiny face. "What do you think, my sweet boy? Are you a Nash?"

David furrowed his brow. "My son, Nash. Hmm. I'm not sure."

"I kind of like Reed."

"Reed? What do you think, buddy?"

Our baby drank on, staring up at me with big eyes.

"I think he only cares about milk," I said. "How about John? For Johnny Cash."

"Cool idea. You don't think it sounds a little old?"

"I honestly don't know. My brain is a murky mess." I thought it over. "It's not like we need to rush into naming him or anything. We can get to know him a little better. See what his personality is like and maybe get a feel for the right name. I don't think he'll mind being called baby for a couple of days."

David's wide smile was a sight to see. "Sounds like a plan. We're doing great as parents. No need to worry about anything, okay?"

Chapter Two

We only had to stay in the hospital for two nights. I was relieved to get home and start putting things in context. Normalizing the situation. There was a lot of talk from medical professionals about how fortunate we were that despite no neonatal care, the baby was healthy and the birth had gone relatively smoothly.

I also had a long discussion with a therapist. Which might need to happen again, depending on how I handled the trauma of the birth long-term. How I actually felt about all of it remained a mystery. But at least I'd stopped bursting into tears every hour or so.

Everyone visited to say hi to the new arrival. The hospital suite quickly filled up with flowers. And while I'd done my best to stay off social media and stay away from the crazy, I couldn't help but hear about some of the things being said. And many of them were unkind and unnecessary.

"I don't want him thinking he wasn't wanted just because he wasn't planned," I said, fussing with the baby blanket.

"He's not going to think that." David pushed my wheelchair while I carefully cradled our swaddled son as the elevator descended, delivering us to our doom. Maybe going home wasn't the answer. Hiding out in the hospital for another day or two might work well. But no, that was quitter's talk. I knew things would be better in our own space. David gave me a grim smile. "Try and relax, baby."

"There's how many paparazzi and fans waiting outside?"

"Everything's going to be okay."

"That's not an answer," I mumbled with a pained laugh. My body felt bloated and leaking, but everything would be okay. It would be.

The two big buff bodyguards, Ziggy and Bon, stood ready and waiting. And there'd be more waiting to see us safely through to the vehicle. Sam had run through everything with us earlier.

While I'd gotten used to handling the spotlight over the last seven years, letting any of that near our child did not appeal to me. Despite starting rumors about our exit happening via a back door and stationing a bodyguard and decoy vehicle there, some people were still loitering near our true exit point. Dammit. We moved out of the elevator, and I put on my big dark sunglasses. A trick my best friend Lauren taught me early on. Ziggy took point walking in front of us while Bon watched our backs.

The flashes were blinding, and the questions being shouted at us were overwhelming.

"Evelyn, did you really not know you were pregnant?"

"Is it true you were in denial about the baby?"

"How does it feel to be the cause of canceling the tour?"

Anything that might cause a reaction, that's what they yelled. Assholes.

When someone got too close, I all but growled at them. A tiny wail came from the baby, and I wanted to bitch slap all of them. So this is what it felt like to get my mama bear on. Because how dare they upset my child. Regardless, we all kept moving briskly toward our waiting SUV.

We climbed into the vehicle quickly. The car door slammed shut, and thank God that was done with. For the time being, at least.

David placed the baby in the infant car seat thingy and had him secured in no time. Which was impressive. "Jimmy gave me lessons. I buckled in one of the twins' teddy bears about a hundred times before the girls okayed me to do it on a real baby. They're pretty hardcore taskmasters."

"Nice. Love me some strong women," I said, relaxing back against the seat. With the windows tinted, we had a modicum of privacy, at least. "I'm so ready to go home."

"Me too. If I had to sleep on that chair one more night…"

The car started moving, and apparently our little one liked the motion. Any and all crying stopped, and he stared wide-eyed at the ceiling. Though it's not like babies can see much at his age. I'd managed some Internet research over the past day. Not enough to make up for nine or so months' worth of preparation and study, but it was a start.

"Can you believe they just let you walk out with a baby?" I smiled. "We only have a vague notion of what we're doing. We could spiral at any moment."

"Speak for yourself. My diaper changing skills are perfection."

"You've come a long way in two days. I'm impressed."

"Thank you." He gave me a tired smile. Truth be known, David seemed to be handling this sudden parenting challenge better than me. He even managed to give our still unnamed son a bath this morning. "You worried about not having a doctor or nurse nearby?"

I sighed. "Logically, I know we're going to be fine. I've just never been in charge of a little human before. What if something happens…like if he gets some tiny sore or something and we don't notice and then it gets infected and—"

"Ev," he said, voice firm.

"I'm borrowing trouble, aren't I?"

"Just a little," he said. "You're going to drive yourself crazy if you start imagining that bad things are waiting around every corner."

"You have a point."

"We're two reasonably capable and intelligent adults. Things are going to be okay."

"Yes," I agreed, shoving aside my mountain of doubts. I took a deep breath and let it out slowly as Portland slipped by outside.

"Everything's going to be okay."

* * * *

"The thing about babies is, they're either hungry, tired, bored, need a diaper change, or have gas." Lena shrugged. "You've just got to correctly guess which one, or which combination, is currently ruining their entire existence."

"You make it sound so easy," I mumbled around a yawn. Four and a half hours of interrupted sleep a night will do that to you. It was amazing we hadn't worn a path up and down the hallway during the many hours a night we walked back and forth, rubbing the baby's back. I now understood why sleep deprivation is a form of torture. I also had a greater empathy for cows. Just call me the Dairy Queen. Making milk was now my life's work. But how amazing was it that I'd made a baby too?

Life could sure come at you fast.

"I have no idea how you managed two at the same time, Lena." Anne relaxed on the couch with a bottle of water in her hand.

"The girls ran Jimmy and me ragged for the first year," said Lena, rubbing my still unnamed son's back. He lay on his stomach across one of her thighs. The child was outraged. Again. Little fists waved, and even his tuft of dark hair seemed to be standing to attention. For someone so small, he sure did give being cranky his everything.

"He's tearing my heart apart," I said.

"Yeah. They're manipulative little suckers," said Lena. "But he'll wear himself out eventually."

Anne just smiled. "They learn how to go to sleep in the womb with all of the movement and the sound of your heart beating. Then they get out, and it's all different, and they don't know how to chill. There wasn't much room in there by the end, so he's used to being contained. All of a sudden he can fling a limb around and startle himself awake."

David and the rest of the band were at a business meeting at Ben and Lizzy's place, a sprawling mansion just outside of the city. They'd even built a recording studio on the property. And their son, Gibson, loved to play in the pool during the summer. Maybe one day we'd move into a house to give us more room. To give our child a backyard to play in and so on. Though I'd miss being in the heart of the Pearl District and so close to work. Not that I'd even managed to get back to the coffee shop since giving birth. Another thing to feel guilty about. Ugh. Women really tended to heap expectations on themselves. Trying to be everything for everyone, all of the time. It was crazy.

On the other hand, I'd never felt such love. I loved my husband. David was the love of my life. But my heart seemed to have doubled to make room for our son. My sweet precious boy. It was nothing short of amazing how much I felt for him. The lengths I would go to for him. Being a mother was wild.

Lena rubbed the palm of her hand in round motions against his tiny back, and ever so slowly, the caterwauling eased and then gradually stopped. The quiet was nothing less than magical. For a moment, all I could hear was our breathing. And all I could feel was a sense of relief.

"He's asleep?" I whispered.

"For now." Lena nodded. "Try not to lower the volume around him too much or he'll never go to sleep unless everything is perfectly silent. And you don't want that. He needs to adapt to your lifestyle a little. Learn to handle the outside world."

"That's true," said Anne. "I hope you don't mind us shoving advice at you."

"Have at it. I need all the help I can get." I rested my head on the back of the sofa. Because the nursery was now the place in the apartment to be.

It had a three-seater sofa in a charcoal material along with a super comfortable rocking chair. The walls were decorated with a vintage-style pale blue sky and fluffy white clouds. And the white antique-looking metal crib was just dreamy. If only my boy would sleep for longer than an hour and a half at a time. That would be amazing. We'd been home for a week now, and life with our pride and joy was not getting any easier. We sort of had a routine, but not really. Not that we didn't have it better than some people. Not that we weren't blessed just by us all being healthy. It was, however, still damn hard.

You'd think that the difficulty of it all would have been less of a surprise to me since I'd watched so many of our friends go through it. But no. Guess it was one of those things I had to experience to understand. Parenthood was no joke.

"You guys did such an amazing job with this room," I said, for not the first time.

"That was mostly Anne." Lena smiled. "She's got the mad decorating and organizing skills."

"It was fun." Anne smiled back at her. "Any luck with the baby names?"

"Nothing seems to quite fit him." I frowned. "We were thinking about Cash and Angus and Reed. But we can't decide on one. We even tried calling him Malcolm. He yawned at us, then he spit up some milk."

"Harsh, but fair," said Lena.

"If it's not right…" Anne just shrugged. "Something will come to you. There's no rush."

I snorted. "With the way we're going, he'll be applying to college as Baby Ferris."

Lena laughed. The baby flinched but stayed asleep. Thank God.

"All of these things people spend their pregnancy thinking about," said Anne. "You didn't get any of that time. Extend yourself some grace, Ev."

"I still feel bad for not knowing," I confessed. "I'll probably always feel bad about that."

"You're not the only person it's happened to. I did some research. One woman I read about had no bump, was still on contraceptives, and fit into all of her clothes the whole way through."

"And you didn't even look pregnant," said Lena. "I saw you every few days or so the month before you had him. There was no big belly or anything to give it away. Your breasts were bodacious, but hey, they always are."

"You notice my breasts?" I asked.

She gave me a wink. "You know it, girl. You rock my world."

I laughed quietly. But the doubt and anxiety still remained, dammit.

Anne grabbed my hand. "I repeat, extend yourself some grace, Evelyn."

"None of us are perfect," said Lena. "And being a mom is damn hard."

"That's a really good point." Anne rubbed her thumb over my knuckles. "Think about it, Ev. Being hard on yourself, especially right now, is unfair. There's no way you'd tolerate that kind of behavior from anyone else. Dealing with a newborn is incredibly difficult. And on top of that, you just gave birth."

"They did tell me it usually takes up to a year to physically and emotionally recover from that," I said.

Anne gave me a gentle smile. "There you go. If you're not going to listen to us, then listen to the people with medical degrees."

I nodded, giving her fingers a squeeze. "Thank you for putting up with my whining."

Lena grinned. "Anytime."

* * * *

Anne was giving the baby a bath when I woke up hours later. Marvelous hours full of much-needed sleep. Thank fuck for friends and found family. The city lights shone bright outside, and my head was clearer, my body lighter and energized. "Hey there. I haven't felt this good in ages. Thank you again for staying."

"You needed the sleep. You're looking a lot better." She lifted the baby out of the little bath set up on the dining room table and wrapped him in a waiting towel. "And I'm happy to help. Tommy doesn't slow down long enough for lots of cuddles these days. He's all go all the time like his father."

"I bet."

"Hello, Cash," she said. "Is that your name? Do you like that one?"

My son's little pink tongue made an appearance.

Anne frowned. "I'm not sure what that means. It could be yummy or it might be a rejection."

"He's going to have his name for the rest of his life," I said. "I don't want to get it wrong."

"It's a big decision." She put the diaper on him before buttoning his onesie. "Nothing smells like a newborn. So soft and tiny. Aren't you, precious one?"

"You miss having a baby?"

"It's a big decision." She sighed. "It feels like we've only just gotten things under control with Tommy. Like we've finally gotten a handle on the situation. Adding a child will be like throwing a hand grenade into the mix. They're such hard work. But I do want another."

I nodded.

"Though it does get easier, Ev."

"I believe you."

Lena left earlier to go to work, leaving Anne here to help. Lena had a photo shoot at a new bar in town. Which just went to show that life didn't have to be all about being a mother. You could also have a career. Achieve things for yourself. Being a mom wouldn't always be quite this demanding, which was good news. As much as I loved my son, I still wanted to be me and have my own interests and have time for my husband. Heck, there was a lot to think about. My brain had been scrambling to keep up since the baby appeared. Guess it was partly a result of nil preparation.

He stared up at Anne with his big blue eyes. Hopefully they'd stay blue like his father's. I think our son was a pretty even mix of David and me, but it was hard to say who he really took after. Time would tell. His mouth worked like he had a lot to say but couldn't quite get it out, so he'd settle for blowing bubbles. And my heart felt about two times too big for my chest.

"I can't wait to see him smile," I said with a grin.

"Oh, yeah," gushed Anne. "And to hear his first word."

"Yeah. Talking of people needing to bathe, which we weren't really," I said, "do you mind if I have a quick shower?"

"No. Go for it. We're good here." Anne smiled at the baby. "Aren't we, Reed? Is your name Reed? What do you think of that one?"

My son just blinked and sucked on his little fist.

"I'm not sure he's down with it." I smoothed his little tuft of soft dark hair back. "We'll figure out a name for you eventually, mystery boy."

"Lizzy said Tommy and Gibson are passed out in front of the TV. So if there's anything you want to get done, I can easily stay for another hour or two."

"Thank you." I smiled. "But David should be home soon. We have plans for trying to catch up with the laundry and maybe cook something for dinner. Though I daresay we'll wind up getting pizza delivered again. Then maybe watch a movie, which we will probably both fall asleep in front of. I tell you, the glamorous rock 'n' roll lifestyle never ends."

Anne laughed.

And suddenly the front door opened and loud yelling filled the condo. Or maybe it was yodeling. It was meant to be some type of singing, I think. The death throes of an extraordinarily hot rock star otherwise known as my husband. He had one arm thrown over Mal's shoulders and the other around Jimmy's. Because he was just that inebriated, apparently. Holy shit. Dark hair hung around his face, and his eyes were tinged red. "Ev."

"Hey," I said, in a not so happy tone of voice.

Jimmy gave me a cautious smile. "They were wetting the baby's head."

"You did what to my child's head?"

"It's a British thing where you celebrate the new arrival with a couple of drinks." Which explained why Jimmy was not under the influence, since he was a recovering alcoholic.

Mal, on the other hand, seemed less than sober. Though he was always sort of high on life, so it could be hard to tell. "It's tradition. We had to!"

Anne closed her eyes tight for a moment. With the baby on her shoulder, she gently patted his back. "Did you happen to notice the part where none of us are in fact British?"

"Bollocks and blimey. What rubbish," said Mal in a horrible attempt at a posh English accent. "Why, I'm as British as...something very British."

"Is that so?"

"Bangers and mash," yelled the blond idiot.

Which scared my son so badly he burst into tears. Give me strength.

"It's okay," I said as Anne passed him to me. "Here we go, sweetie. Everything's fine. Ignore the drunken idiots."

Mal winced. "Sorry, little dude."

"So you had a party, huh?" I asked.

David tried to focus on me, but I'm not sure he was entirely successful given all the blinking involved. "Just a little one."

"You can't even stand on your own, babe."

"Um..." And the scent of scotch was so strong. His breath was pure fumes, just waiting for a flame. What a mess.

Jimmy's gaze was full of apology. As if it were his fault his brother was in this condition. Grownups made their own choices.

"Put him on the couch." I stepped out of the way. "Thank you."

A week ago, it would have been no big deal. Of course, a week ago, it would have been unlikely to happen. The band sometimes had a few drinks together. There was a fair argument to be made that partying was part of the music industry. Celebrating achievements with a bottle of champagne. Shooting tequila before taking to the stage. It happened, but no one got hammered. Not like this. We were all mature responsible adults. Mostly. Okay. So if he did make a big night of it, he'd do it when we had nothing else going on. When a hangover didn't matter.

"I'll take this one home." Anne grabbed Mal's hand and tugged him toward the door with no small amount of determination. "See you later, Ev."

"Bye. And thanks again."

She just nodded.

"But Davie needs me," said Mal.

"Read the room, Malcolm," grouched his wife. "The party is over."

"Oh, yeah. This room does not feel happy. Maybe it needs some fucking Feng Shui or something. What do you—"

And the door shut behind them. Thank God. One disaster (or drunk rock star) at a time was more than enough.

Jimmy frowned. "Ben bought a couple of bottles of some fancy scotch to celebrate the birth. It was only supposed to be a couple of drinks, but it got a bit out of hand."

"Oh," I said.

"I don't feel so good," mumbled David on the couch. His face had indeed gone pale.

"Bucket?" asked Jimmy.

"Grab a plastic container or a big bowl from the kitchen pantry." I pointed the way.

Jimmy ran.

The baby kept fussing because he could smell his food source close by and was hungry. So I set up in my usual lounge chair on the other side of the room. Thank goodness for wrap tops making breastfeeding more accessible. While my son started suckling, I watched my husband turn an alarming shade of green.

Jimmy shoved the big metal bowl at David just in time for him to hurl. Oy vey.

I didn't want to guess how much alcohol it would take to make him this sick. Or how fast he must have downed it. I'd only been asleep for a couple of hours. The band meeting at Ben's house must not have been that long.

Jimmy disappeared again, returning with a wet face cloth, a glass of water, and some Advil. "Do you need anything, Ev?"

"I'm fine. Thanks."

David groaned and sank back onto the couch. "Shit. What the hell was I thinking?"

"Not sure you really were," said Jimmy. "You just kind of cut loose and went for it. Haven't seen you go at it like that in years."

I sighed. "The last week has been pretty hardcore for everyone."

"Can I empty it?" asked Jimmy, pointing to the bowl of doom.

"Yeah, I think I'm okay now." David sipped at the water. "This is good."

Jimmy just nodded.

"Thanks, Jimmy," I said.

"We had plans for tonight," said David in a hoarse voice.

"Yeah."

"I kind of forgot."

I frowned.

"You're mad."

"I honestly don't know what I am," I said, caressing the baby's little hand. "But I think if one of us wants to relax and have a few drinks, that's the sort of thing we need to organize ahead of time now."

He nodded, his forehead furrowed in concentration. Probably to ensure he didn't accidentally fall off the couch or something. There was nothing like high blood alcohol level to enhance your general life skills. And there wasn't any point in saying more. Not that I even knew what to say, my head was a mess. Having a heart-to-heart with him now, when he likely wouldn't remember what we said in the morning, was not appealing. My energy levels just weren't that good.

Neither was my patience, apparently. Thank God Jimmy was here.

"Let's get you in the shower, stinker," said Jimmy, giving his brother a hand.

David laughed drunkenly. "You're making me sound like I'm some annoying little kid."

"That makes sense since you're behaving like a man child right now."

"Ouch," said David, swaying on his feet. "Harsh, dude."

I focused on feeding the baby and said a whole lot of nothing.

Chapter Three

David stumbled out of the spare bedroom at around ten the next morning with a "Hey."

The baby and I were hanging out on the living room floor. He lay on a blanket, staring up at the toys hanging above. The yellow star in particular seemed to call to him. Lord help us if we had another rock star in the making. A second generation of Stage Dive madness would be wild. I wasn't sure the world would survive it.

The baby and I had done our couple of minutes of tummy time. Diapers had been changed, and milk had been consumed. The day was going fine, give or take my inner turmoil.

David wore a pair of sweatpants and nothing else. Normally I'd take a moment to indulge my lust. But any positive feelings toward him were missing this morning. His long dark hair was a veritable bird's nest. Guess Jimmy was willing to only go so far with his caretaking. Fair enough. He cleaned him up and dumped him in the spare room to sleep it off, which was for the best. Nothing snored like a drunk, and I needed all the uninterrupted sleep I could get. So did our son.

"Did you take the Advil I left beside the bed?" I asked.

"Yeah. Thanks. How are you doing?" he asked, leaning against a wall.

"We're okay."

His gaze narrowed. "You're angry, Ev."

"I'm just tired, mostly."

"But you're also pissed at me."

I took a deep breath and let it out slowly. "I think I have a right to be, don't you?"

"I know we had plans for last night, and I'm sorry about that, but…it was just a few drinks with the guys to celebrate."

"Which I had no warning of, and you left me alone to look after our son," I said. "And it wasn't just a few drinks. You were drunk off your ass. I haven't seen you like that in years."

His raised his chin. "Am I not allowed to cut loose now and then?"

"You're allowed to do whatever the hell you want. You're a grown adult. And I know that things have been stressful lately. But I'd ask that you show a little consideration."

He turned away.

"You could have called me and let me know what was happening, at the very least. And you could have crashed at Ben and Lizzy's."

"I wanted to come home," he growled.

"So you could stagger around, throw up, and pass out?" I kept my voice calm so as not to freak out the baby. "We're just lucky Jimmy was here to help."

A muscle jumped in the side of his jaw. "Don't you think you're making a bit too much of this?"

"No. And trust me, I've overthought this to the nth degree all damn night."

He hung his head.

My heart ached for him. Hell, it ached for all of us. What a mess life was. "I know this hasn't been easy, but we have to work together here."

"Baby, I know. I just…"

"You just what?"

"I don't know." He sighed. "I guess I thought it would be more fun having a child and all, you know?"

"Fun?" I asked, stunned. "Are you serious? I get that our lives have been turned upside down with no warning. But I'm recovering from giving birth and trying to look after a baby. I need you to have my back right now whether it's a good time or not."

The baby started to fuss. It was feeding time. Again. And I'm sure he was picking up on the wealth of bad vibes filling the room. They said that babies could sense all sorts of things. I knew I could. I had a list of worries in my mind stretching from here to the moon. Like how every day since we'd gotten home from the hospital David had gotten quieter and quieter, and I'd felt more alone. Doubts seemed to pour into the widening gap between us. Maybe he'd have been happier being back on the road with the band. Maybe he blamed me for having to cancel the tour. Maybe being here with me and our son wasn't what he wanted to do with his life. The anxiety was endless.

What I knew was, he no longer felt like my safe space, my touchstone. All of these emotions were a swirling storm inside of me I didn't know how to deal with. And denial sure wasn't working.

My eyes were open painfully wide. "I can't do this with you right now."

"What?"

"I love you. But I don't have the energy to look after two children. Not when one is supposed to be a grown-ass male."

"The fuck is that supposed to mean?"

I gathered up the baby and got to my feet, went into the nursery, and shut the door. Because anything else I said was just going to make matters worse. And what I said had been pretty damn straightforward. I'd never felt so fragile and alone in my life.

"You're my favorite male right now in the whole wide world," I told my son and kissed his head. "Hands down. The clear winner."

Everything would be fine. One way or another. We'd weather this storm just like we'd weathered the rest. I hoped.

* * * *

The flowers arrived about an hour later. I didn't know where David had gone, but I was glad for the breathing room. And for the sweet scent of peony roses. The baby was fast asleep, and my stress levels were easing back to a more normal level. At least, they were until I opened the card attached to the vase.

I may have behaved inappropriately last night. Love, Mal.

I stared at the gift in surprise. "Huh."

Not from my husband. Okay. A little disappointing, but still nice to receive. I hadn't received flowers since Paris. Damn, that had been a good night. A baby-making night, most likely, given the timing. Now David and I were fighting, and everything was bleh. Though my son was healthy and happy, and that was great. I just wish my husband and I could say the same. About being happy. We were healthy enough, give or take his hangover.

Maybe I should try him on his cell. And say what? We fought a lot in our first year of marriage, but then things calmed down. All of the boundaries had been set. Expectations established, and so on. Guess we needed to go through that again, as a family this time. As new parents.

A knock on the door had me placing the peonies on the table.

"Ma'am," said Harry the doorman. He held two more vases of flowers, one in each arm. Roses and wildflowers. One bouquet was in a crystal vase, the other was in a rustic wooden box. "More arrived when I went back down. Shall I carry them in for you? They're a little heavy."

"Thank you. That would be great." I got out of the man's way as he placed them alongside the first bouquet. This was...unexpected. And I couldn't help the little light in my heart that hoped they were from David this time.

Harry left, and I opened up the next card.

No really. It was my bad. Don't blame yourself. Love, Mal.

I set the card aside and looked to heaven. Malcolm was apparently on a roll. An apologetic one, but still. "Give me strength. I wasn't blaming myself, you fool."

Then I picked up the third, and hopefully last, card. Though getting flowers was kind of great.

Oh, fine. I forgive you. Let's forget it ever happened. Love, Mal.

I laughed and shook my head. Tiredness makes you receptive to the silliest of humor. It's the truth. And this was exactly how the drummer got away with being crazy all the damn time. He was charming despite everything.

Still no sign of or word from David. Which sucked. But I hadn't been in the wrong, and he needed to get with the program. And, oh man. I just wanted everything to be okay. To get everything back under control. Life without a plan was not smooth sailing.

However, one thing motherhood had taught me was to rest when you could. That, and never wake a sleeping baby. Since my hair was already reasonably clean and my black sweats were sort of fresh, I grabbed a pillow and a blanket and made myself comfortable on the couch with the baby monitor. Self-care these days was a whole lot about sleep. Screw the skincare routine. I drank a bottle of water earlier. Good enough. Having a child was basically crossing out the top ten things that were important to you and replacing them with your infant. The one who still needed a name. Eh. One of these days. It wasn't bothering him—yet. And David didn't seem overly interested in the process these days. Our first big decision together about the baby, and he'd opted out. Ouch.

As I slipped off into sleep, I could still feel the uneasy feeling inside me. Hopefully David was taking time to think, and we could talk things through and clear the air when he returned. Hopefully.

* * * *

Muffled yelling woke me. The soundproofing in the condo was hardcore. For me to be able to hear anything from the hallway outside the apartment where the elevators were, someone had to pissed. Big time.

More shouting. And those voices were horribly familiar. I grabbed my cell and the baby monitor and ran for the door. Two men tussled. David grabbed fistfuls of his brother's sweater while Jimmy seemed to be doing his best to hold him off. Not so successfully.

I hit the number for downstairs and said, "Send up security to the penthouse. Now."

"It's none of your fucking business," snarled David.

"Of course it's my fucking business." Jimmy pushed back. "Keep things up like this and you're going to ruin your life."

They careened off a wall and staggered back. It was like rock 'n' roll wrestling come to life, in a horrible manner. Two spots of red sat high on David's cheekbones, rage lighting his eyes. He was full-on losing it. Of all the times to not have security hovering. Holy shit.

"Get your hands off me," ordered Jimmy. "You're behaving like a damn fool."

"Oh, yeah. Jimmy's got all the answers. He knows everything!"

"Davie, I'm warning you…"

"Got his life together and his marriage is perfect. Just ask him."

Jimmy growled. His hands were clenched tight around his brother's wrists. "You're too fucking defensive to take advice. Fine."

"Because I definitely need another person telling me what to do."

"She's right. You're behaving like a child," said Jimmy. "Davie, let me go. Now. I won't ask again."

They didn't even seem to realize they had an audience as they pushed and shoved at each other.

Then Jimmy pulled back an arm, formed a fist, and let it fly. Straight at his brother's face. David's head snapped back from the impact, and his hold released. He stumbled back against the wall, hands covering his eye.

"Oh, no," I said.

Jimmy turned to me and frowned. "Ev… shit."

The elevator dinged, and the doors opened, Bon stepping out.

He took in the scene with a practiced eye and managed to keep a neutral face. Which I appreciated. Then he knelt down in front of David and coaxed him into showing off his nice, fresh black eye. Jesus. I always hated violence. I focused on taking deep, even breaths because hyperventilating wouldn't help.

David got into a fight shortly after we got together, but nothing since. He was a lover, not a fighter. He wasn't angry like this. Not normally. We didn't really live a rock 'n' roll lifestyle. No drugs apart from the occasional joint. No craziness apart from Mal. And definitely no trashing places and shouting the house down. Sure, there was the occasional party or get-together or a drink after a show when the guys were on tour. But nothing like this.

"I'm sorry, Ev," said Jimmy.

"I know." I nodded. "It's probably best if you go for now."

With a sad smile, he disappeared into the elevator and left.

"How badly is he hurt, Bon?" I asked.

"Nothing a pack of ice won't fix. But I can get a doctor over if you'd like to be sure."

"David?"

"I'm fine." He didn't look up. "Don't need a doctor."

"Are you drunk again?" I asked in my calmest possible voice.

"No," he growled.

What the hell else was I supposed to think when he started brawling with his brother? Give me strength.

"I need you to calm down, please," I said, face set.

My husband looked at me and sighed. Slowly but surely, his shoulders fell back to a more normal level. All of that rage was leaving his body. "Okay."

"I think we're okay now, Bon. Right, David?"

"Yeah," said David, staring at the floor with his one good eye.

"Thank you, Bon."

The bodyguard looked between us, then nodded and pushed the button for the elevator.

"Let's go get that ice." I headed back into the apartment, making for the kitchen. Heavy footsteps followed behind me. My hands shook, but I could ignore that. I grabbed a kitchen towel and filled it with the cold stuff before handing it to him.

"Got another lecture for me?" he asked sullenly.

"Nope."

He scoffed. "That'd be a change. Jimmy's been going off on me for the last fucking hour."

I kept my mouth shut.

With half of his face covered, he looked at me. "Say something."

"I don't know what to say."

His Adam's apple bobbed. "You always know what to say. It's like your specialty."

"Okay," I said. "How about, I don't know what to say that won't set you off again. And I see no point in having another argument or...I don't know. Guess I already said everything I had to say this morning. Not that it helped."

Hurt filled his gaze, but he said nothing.

From the monitor came a tiny wail. The baby was awake.

David flinched.

"I hate this. You and Jimmy fighting. You and me being all messed up." A sob caught in my throat, and I wrapped my arms tight around myself. Tears streamed down my face. There was nothing I could do to stop them. I didn't even try.

A stark expression crossed his face. "Ev."

As much as I wanted to reach out and touch him, it didn't feel safe. Not that I thought he'd physically hurt me. But there was a wall between us now. One I didn't know how to begin to take down.

"Ev," he said, voice tortured. "Please don't cry."

"I need you to fix it, David. Because you're mine and I love you and you're the only one who can fix it, all right?"

After a moment, he nodded. "All right."

"Good. Okay. I'm gonna go check on our son." And I got the hell out of there.

When I came back out, he was gone. Again.

* * * *

Lizzy arrived an hour later holding a cake. "Am I the first to arrive?"

"Huh?" I kept on burping the baby on my shoulder. "What's going on?"

"You didn't think we'd actually respect your privacy and leave you alone during this difficult time, did you?" She bustled on into the kitchen. "You know us better than that."

"Jimmy told Lena," I said, making the connection.

"He sure did. And then she told all of us."

My shoulders sagged. "I'm not sure I'm very good company right now."

She held out her hands. "Give me the baby."

I handed him over.

"Hey there, little one," said Lizzy. "Aren't you just the cutest?"

I followed behind her as she strode on out to the living room and made herself at home. With my small child in tow. She stood over by the windows, rocking back and forth. And he gurgled happily. What a traitor. He'd screamed at me for the past half an hour for reasons known only to himself. Maybe in reaction to my bad mood. Parenthood was no joke.

"Did I ever tell you about the time I kicked Ben out of the house?" she asked, still making kissy faces at my son.

I settled into the corner of the sofa with an emotional support cushion in my lap. "No."

"Oh, yeah. It was about…a year ago. Give or take."

My eyebrows shot up.

She laughed quietly. "Did you think you were the only one experiencing the occasional relationship hiccup?"

"But you're basically a qualified therapist."

"Nearly," she agreed. "And I still kick that man out on his ass when he is being an ass."

I just blinked.

"It's one of the reasons I made sure our place had a pool house, actually." She smiled wistfully. "So Ben wouldn't have far to go."

"What did he do?" I asked. "Or shouldn't I ask?"

She shrugged. "He gets fixated on the music and needs a reminder about priorities occasionally. Work is great. But family and a healthy relationship is important. So yeah… I tend to kick him out about once a year just to make sure everything's going smoothly. Give us a chance to air grievances and clear up misunderstandings. We whisper yell at each other so Gibby doesn't hear. Then Ben spends a night in the pool house. Or about half a night. He usually creeps in around two or three in the morning to grovel and have make-up sex."

My eyebrows felt about halfway up my forehead. "Wow."

"Everyone's relationship works differently."

There came another knock at the door, and I rushed to open it. Anne and Lena stood there loaded down with takeout and bottles of wine.

"Oh, that smell." I breathed deep with relish. "I know that smell. I love that smell."

"We got Chinese," said Anne. "I hope that was the right call."

And I didn't burst into tears. One little bastard just happened to escape, is all. Hormones. It had been one of hell of a day. "Thank you. I love pizza, but I've eaten a lot of it lately. Chinese sounds wonderful."

Lena smacked a kiss on my cheek. "C'mon, Evelyn. Don't cry over takeout. We've got you. You're all good, lady."

I sniffled.

"I was just telling her about kicking out Ben," said Lizzy.

Anne snorted. "Well…it works or you wouldn't do it. I tried to kick Mal out once and he staged a sit-in. He had a protest banner saying love me and everything."

Lena headed into the kitchen.

"What did you do?" I asked.

"After he groveled for a suitable amount of time I forgave him."

She shrugged. Then she fetched wine glasses out of the wooden bar cabinet. "He learned his lesson. At least, I think he did. With him it can be hard to tell. But he doesn't tend to make the same mistake twice."

"Not to be annoying, but honestly, David and I don't usually fight. So this has kind of thrown me. I don't even know where he is right now. I sent him a text, asking if he was okay, and nothing." I arranged the Chinese takeout containers on the coffee table. My mouth was watering. Misery loves dumplings, apparently.

"I've got an update," said Lena, emerging from the kitchen with plates and silverware. "Jimmy just texted me. David is at our place."

"He is?"

Lena nodded. "And he is apparently very subdued. They're talking things through."

"Thank God."

"They're brothers." Anne smiled. "They'll work it out."

"It's true. The sibling bond is tight but occasionally fractious," said Lizzy. "For example, Anne used to pull my hair."

"I did not!"

"Oh you did so. Be honest."

Anne frowned. "Fine. But it was only that one time when you gave my favorite doll a haircut."

"And she looked amazing with a fauxhawk."

Anne just sighed and started serving herself some crispy duck.

"I can't talk," said Lena. "My sister stole my loser boyfriend and married him. Though that only lasted two years. Not a surprise. She's happy with an older man now. He indulges her every whim. I could have told her she was narcissistic and needed a sugar daddy. Pretty sure I did, actually. But the point I'm making is, families are weird."

"I hear you." I loaded up a plate. "My dad still likes to name drop divorce lawyers during family dinners sometimes. Just to keep David on his toes, apparently."

"Yikes," said Lizzy, rocking the baby.

"I'm not hungry." Anne held out her arms to him. "I'll take him while you eat."

"Why aren't you hungry?"

"Just feeling a bit off. No big deal."

Lizzy narrowed her eyes on her sister as she handed the infant over. "Anne, is there something you'd like to share with the group?"

"No."

"How about a glass of wine?"

"Not right now. Maybe later." Anne settled the baby over her shoulder. "Thank you."

Her sister did not look pacified. "Hmm."

Lena and I exchanged a glance, but said not a word. Whatever was going on with Anne was her own business. Though why we gave her privacy when they were all up in my business, I don't know. Not that I wasn't glad to have them all there. Being surrounded by my friends made things instantly better. Along with knowing David and Jimmy were talking things through.

Guess respecting a friend's privacy had a lot to do with giving that friend what they needed in that particular moment. And cross your fingers you didn't get it wrong. Every relationship was tricky. They all took work.

"Thank you for being here, you guys," I said to one and all. "I really mean it. This would have been so much more difficult to handle alone. I feel like David is just opting out of our life together. Like the idea of being a family doesn't appeal. He hardly talks to me. Won't discuss a name for the baby. He just...I don't know."

Anne frowned. "That sounds really hard."

"Yeah." I sighed. "I'm worried this is going to be the end of us. And I don't know what to do."

Lena moved to my side and slipped an arm around my shoulders. "One thing at a time, Ev. Eat now. You have to look after yourself so you can look after the baby. Then we'll come up with a plan for dealing with your fool of a husband."

"Okay." I sniffed. "Thank you."

She smiled. "Anytime."

Chapter Four

David: I need a couple of days.

Me: For what?

David: Just to sort things out. Ok?

Me: We always said we'd face things together.

David: Ev, I can't. I need the space to fix things on my own this time.

Me: I don't even know what to say. Ok I guess. You're not giving me any other options.

Me: I don't like it, but if that's what you need.

David: Thank you. I love you.

Me: I love you too.

I sat at the table with the baby monitor, staring into space. How many different ways could your heart break? That was the question. It felt like mine had been entrusted to the wrong person suddenly. David and I had always had each other's backs. We'd always done our best to be there for each other and now…he wasn't coming home. Not yet at least. Maybe not ever. And I hated not knowing as much as I hated him not being here.

Head in my hands, I sat and cried.

* * * *

The call came from the front desk just after two the next afternoon. "Mrs. Ferris? A Jude Darcy is here to see you. She says she was sent by Mr. Ferris."

"Um, all right. Send her up," I said. "Thank you."

A young blonde woman was standing at my door a couple of minutes later. She had blunt edgy bangs and a nose piercing. "Mrs. Ferris. Hello. It's lovely to meet you."

"Hi," I said, bewildered. "My husband sent you?"

"Yes. I met with him and his associates this morning. And it was agreed that so long as you're happy with the arrangements, I was to start work immediately."

She was smiling at me, so I smiled at her and… "Huh?"

Her smile dimmed. "Ah, I'm your new housekeeper slash nanny. If you'll have me. I have a printout of my resume for you in my handbag. And of course I've already signed an N.D.A. and so on."

"You're my new housekeeper slash nanny?" I stared off at nothing. "Wow."

The woman held a small bundle of papers in her hands. "They didn't tell you?"

"Not a word."

"Okay. What's the best way to handle this…let me think." She took a deep breath. "Hi, my name is Jude Darcy. I'm twenty-five years old. Born and bred in this fair city. I've worked for the last two years for a well-known family down in Los Angeles. So I'm familiar with dealing with celebrities and fans and security and so on. I have references, and you're very welcome to give them a call and check for yourself."

"Did my husband already do that?"

"No. A person by the name of Martha, I believe."

"And she was happy with you?" My eyebrows rose. "You must be good. Okay. Carry on."

"Can I ask a question?"

"Go ahead."

"Do I really have to become proficient on the drums as part of this position? I'm pretty sure that was a joke, but I just want to make sure."

"Malcolm Ericson was at your interview."

"Yes."

I nodded. "No, you wouldn't have to learn the drums."

"And the speaking fluent Greek and fire twirling…"

"Likewise, unnecessary."

"Got it," she said. "Phew."

"Come on in, Jude. Let's talk."

"Let me first ask: Are you open to having someone help out?" She gave me a small smile. "If not, I don't want to waste your time. I realize this has been sprung on you."

"It sure has." I took a moment and thought it over. I should probably be furious that all of this was organized behind my back. But honestly, why bother? Who had the energy? When (not if) David came home, we weren't going to suddenly magically start coping. Stress was a big problem. For him and me. We could afford the help, so why not?

I wouldn't be less of a woman or mother or whatever because someone was picking up the slack in the condo and helping with the baby. If she was the right person to let into our home. It was a risk. She was pretty, if not beautiful, and much more pleasant to be around right now than me. I mean, she actually had the energy to wear makeup and coordinate outfits. Even if that outfit was just jeans and a button-down shirt. And I bet her boobs didn't leak.

But I trusted David. He regularly travelled without me and had women throwing themselves at him. And we wouldn't know if having her around would help unless we tried. "The fact is, I think we could really use some assistance."

The woman beamed. "Great."

Me: House Keeper/Nanny?

David: What do you think?

Me: We should have discussed it first. But I like her and it is a good idea.

David: Good. We were lucky to get her. One of the bodyguards met her on a job and was impressed. She was thinking of taking a position in France.

Me: How'd you talk her into it?

David: Left it up to Martha and Jimmy.

Me: And money?

David: There was a healthy signing bonus.

Me: When are you coming home?

David: Soon. Just give me another day or so. I promise I'm working on things.

Me: Like what? I need more than that. Please. We're feeling pretty damn abandoned here.

David: I know and I'm sorry. My head isn't where it should be. I'm going to fix it and get back to you as soon as I can.

Me: You're talking to someone?

David: Yes. I'm getting help.

Me: Ok

Me: Any ideas for our son's name yet?

David: No. Is he ok?

Me: Yeah he's good. He misses you.

David: I love you.

Me: I love you too.

I first realized I was low key in love with Jude Darcy the next day. She was folding laundry with the baby lying on a rug nearby. Jude was quietly singing *Nine to Five* by Dolly Parton, and the scent of something delicious filled the air. The condo didn't look like a bomb had hit it. What a miracle. The woman was magic. We had someone in to clean the condo once a week. But you could amass a lot of mess in that time.

"You've been cooking?" I asked.

She smiled. "Just chicken pot pie and a garden salad. Nothing fancy."

"Yum. I'll take it." At the sound of my voice, the baby started fussing and sucking on his little fist. "You're hungry too, huh?"

"He seems pretty chill, as far as babies go."

"You think so?" I picked him up and settled us in an armchair for feeding time. Along with my bottle of water and cell. Being able to hydrate and having something to do if he decided to mess around and take all day were both necessary for my sanity. I smoothed back his tuft of dark hair. His skin was so soft and had that baby smell. My beautiful little boy.

Jude kept folding the laundry.

"Does it bother you, handling our underwear?" I asked. "I hadn't thought about it before, but if you're not comfortable–"

"It's fine," she said. "At one job, I had to iron everything. His boxers and her briefs and the bed sheets and you name it. So just folding and putting everything away is easy."

"You had to iron their underwear? Now that's high maintenance."

"I shouldn't be gossiping."

"No names have been mentioned."

"Nor will they be. I do know how to keep my mouth shut, I promise."

I smiled.

Of course, it was a concern. The media was always open to new, scandalous tales about us. Me and my surprise baby gave them enough to talk about for the time being, thank you very much. But Martha wouldn't have let Jude into our home if she wasn't certain of her discretion. Martha was David's first girlfriend way back when. Then she'd been the band's assistant for several years. Now she successfully managed a couple of up and coming rock acts. She was also Ben the bass player's sister. And the woman was a barracuda when it came to protecting those she considered family. We mostly got along. It kind of depended on how hardcore her mood was at the time. However, I definitely trusted her when it came to something like this. I'm sure she vetted Jude to heck and back. It was nice not to have to worry about it, honestly.

If it had been up to me to pick someone to come into our home and help, I'd have been a mess of nerves. There wasn't room in my brain to deal with anything extra these days. Let alone decide on someone who would have access to my child. I was grateful David and everyone stepped in and found me an angel.

I ran a finger back and forth over the back of his little fingers as he drank his dinner. It both was and wasn't weird to not have David here. He often travelled with the band, so not having him here wasn't unusual. But it was like a dark storm cloud hanging over me and our son. The knowledge that things had gone so badly that he had to step back from our life together. Though he hadn't stepped back, exactly. Actually, I wasn't quite sure what he was doing. But everything felt sad and edgy and just generally off. Which sucked.

* * * *

David came home the next afternoon. Keys in hand, black jeans and Henley on, he stood near the entry. "Okay if I come in?"

My breath caught in my throat as I stared at him. Talk about a sight for sore eyes. And a sore heart. The organ currently felt like it was trying to beat itself right out of my chest. I honestly didn't know whether to hug him or slap him. I'd missed him so much, but his being gone had been hell. The last few days had been some of the worst of my life. And his eyes were wounded, his face leaner and starker somehow. As if this time had aged us both. I curled my hands into fists and kept them at my side. We needed to talk. That's what had to come first.

"Of course you can come in," I said.

Jude had left for the day, and the baby was sleeping. I'd made myself a cup of decaf coffee and decided to sit and chill on the sofa.

He took a chair opposite me. Which felt ominous for some reason. Like he needed the coffee table between us. His black eye was a combination of dark purple and gray. Gruesome. "Jimmy got me in with a therapist. That's what I've been doing the last couple of days. Mostly."

"Okay."

"We talked about a lot of things."

I nodded, trying to ignore the doubts and feelings of dread curling inside my stomach. Everything would be fine. I wouldn't let it be anything else.

"Like how I'm not really used to sharing your attention. Or dealing with you just not having the time and energy for me or our relationship right now," he said. "And of course that's perfectly understandable. You're exhausted. Hell. We both are."

"Do you resent the baby, David?"

"A little."

I took a deep breath and let it out slowly. No wonder our baby still didn't have a name.

"I'm also kind of freaking out about how we're going to deal with all this. How we're going to balance things. Our life's been upended." He swallowed. "I love him, Ev. But he's a handful."

"Yeah."

His hands hung loose, his forearms braced on his spread legs. And those tattoos on his fingers spelling out LIVE FREE had never seemed more pertinent. Because he couldn't live free anymore, and neither could I. Now we were parents.

"It's a big sacrifice," I said. "And I know they keep saying it'll get easier. But we have to be here living it day in and out."

He nodded. "How's Jude doing?"

"She's great. Having her here has really helped."

"Good. That's good, Ev." His gave me a small smile. "I've also been looking at houses."

"You want to move?" I asked, surprised. "Whoa. That's not what I expected you to say. I mean, I thought you loved this place.

We've been so happy here."

"I know," he said, keeping his voice calm and certain. If he hadn't practiced saying these words, then he'd thought about them a whole lot. "It's a big ask. But I feel like there's not enough room here for all of us anymore. Not with all of the baby stuff and people sleeping at different times and me worrying about playing music and disturbing someone. I want us all to have enough space. All three of us."

"Okay. If that's what you want."

"I know this is close to your work, but—"

"No. I agree." I smiled. It was mostly natural. "It might take me a little while to get used to the idea, but we all need to be comfortable in our own home. Being here has been great, but…we're moving into a new phase of our life now. We can afford it, and hopefully it will help with things, so why not?"

"Yeah. That's what I think too."

"What else did the therapist say?"

"She said that for new parents self-doubt and even anger at how you feel you've lost control over your life are normal. Ten to fifteen percent of new dads have issues with that sort of thing. Anxiety and mood disorders and so on."

"That's a lot."

"And she said the worst thing I can do is stop communicating."

"We need to make more of an effort to talk," I agreed.

"Yeah. Otherwise the bitterness and resentment can get out of control. She also said it's okay to mourn the fact that, for a while at least, we can't just do what we want. Life has kind of moved on. We can't just drop everything and go to Maui. Decide on the spur of moment to go hear a band play at some club together." He looked away for a moment. "You know I'm in this with you to the end, right?"

And hearing those words unlocked something inside of me. Some hurt or worry. "I know."

"Good."

"Did she say anything else?"

"That you should think about doing therapy too. Both with me and on your own." He swallowed. "The thing is, I walked out on you and our son, Ev. And I'm never going to be able to apologize enough for that. No matter that I needed to get my shit together, that I was going through some stuff. It's pretty damn unforgivable. Me getting drunk and fighting and shutting you out. It was bullshit behavior, and I'm so damn sorry. Please know that."

"Yes," I agreed. "That was…even if I understand why you did it, it's a lot."

"You've just had a baby, and you're dealing with even more than me, I know. Me adding this stress on top of everything was fucked."

I nodded dully.

"I'm just asking for a chance to get us back on track. To make it up to you and him." He stared into my eyes intently. "And if you don't want the nanny or the new house or any of it, then okay. We'll find another way to deal with things together. I just want to be here with you and our son. Please."

I took a deep breath and let it out slowly. My emotions were running riot. My head spinning in circles. This was a lot. "I need a little time to think everything over, but…mostly I think I'm all right with your ideas."

"Of course. Take whatever time you need. I'm not going anywhere again, I promise."

"What else did the therapist say?"

His eyes opened wide. "She said a lot. We talked for hours. I had a lot of shit in my head I just needed to get out, you know? Then I could start trying to fix things. Get with the program and have your back the way I should."

I smiled.

"I'm sorry this happened, baby."

"Sounds like it's outside of your control. We can't dictate our feelings. They just happen. But you're dealing with it. That takes courage."

He nodded. "I didn't want to disappear on you. But I didn't want to make things worse either. And then I felt guilty for all of it, and it was just a fucking mess."

"I know."

"We'll handle things together from now on," he said. "I'm going to keep seeing the therapist and keep on top of any of this shit."

"Good."

"And I know moving is a pain in the ass. But I figure, if you want, we can keep this place. Buy another lot of whatever we need and have it all ready to go at the new place. Wherever that winds up being." His fingers tapped a beat against his leg. "All of the money's got to be useful for something, right?"

I nodded and relaxed back against the couch. Deep, even breaths. We were going to be okay. "And it's not like anyone else would want to live next to Mal."

"That's very true." His smile came more quickly this time. Seemed more normal. The stiffness in his body seemed to also be slowly easing. "She talked about support groups for new parents. But given how well known we are and everything, it didn't seem like a good idea."

"That would be a big risk."

"Enough of our life gets splashed across the Internet."

"Agreed."

He slumped back in the seat.

"Are things okay with Jimmy?"

"I apologized for being an ass. He said he regretted having to punch me, but it was for the greater good."

I snorted. "That sounds like your brother."

"Yeah." He gave a slight smile and then sobered. His focus entirely aimed at me. "I was an ass, Ev. To Jimmy, yeah, but most of all, to you. And our son. I missed time with you both. I made you worry. And I was so up in my head, I hurt you. The last thing I'd ever want to do. I'm sorry, baby. I need you, now and always. I need you both. Will you forgive me?"

And if I could have nuked the beautiful heavy wooden coffee table out of existence, I would have. But instead, I got up and walked around it and climbed into David's lap. A place I'd needed to be for quite some time now. "I need some serious cuddling."

"That would be great." He wrapped his arms tight around me.

I rested my head against his shoulder and breathed in the warmth and familiar scent of his skin. Because it was totally okay to hide from the world with my husband for a minute. We were together. We were good.

"Are you crying?" he asked, tone bewildered.

"Hush." I slapped a hand over his mouth. "Like I said, these last few days have been a lot. And then there's the hormones. Crying is like my hobby now."

With care, he removed my hand and pressed a kiss to the top of my head. "Love you, baby. We're going to get through this."

"We will," I agreed, sniffling. "We definitely will."

Chapter Five

"Do we really need a heli-pad and a cigar room?" I asked, sipping on an OJ.

David sat strumming his guitar with our son lying beside him on a rug. And the baby was staring at him (or the general vicinity from where the sounds were coming) with wonder. It was gorgeous to see.

The last few weeks had been a bit easier going. With Jude helping and David and I both going to therapy, life was calmer. He was now one hundred and ten percent committed to our family. We talked a lot and hugged a lot and generally made more of an effort with each other and our small family. I was even getting better at putting the baby to sleep. My swaddling skills were second to none. I'd also started working out how to express milk so I could go into work for a few hours now and then to deal with any big issues. Also to feel like I did still have a life outside the home if I wanted one. Energy levels permitting, of course. Fortunately for all, the café had excellent staff. And lining up some houses to look at next week with a real estate agent was kind of fun. Much more fun than talking about diapers and so on. Moving was big, but I thought we could work it out so things went smoothly.

Mal scrolled through properties on his cell. "Are you crazy? You definitely need a cigar room."

I gave him a look most skeptical.

"If you two are going to abandon me, you've got to make it worth it."

"I wonder if this is really all about you," said Anne, tone contemplative.

"Pumpkin." He shook his head. "That is not being supportive."

We were hanging out at Lena and Jimmy's house for a change of pace. Apart from medical appointments, it was the first real outing we'd attempted. Leaving the apartment for a while was great. Even if we did bring everything including the kitchen sink. The contents of the baby bag covered all seasons and weather eventualities and the baby's next four stages of development. Roughly. It was nice to get almost everyone together. Ben, Liz, and Gibby were currently vacationing in Fiji. Lucky them.

"You don't want to build?" asked Lena.

"It would take too long," I said. "And I don't really feel like we have the energy right now."

"Fair enough."

Anne lay on the opposite sofa. "You can always build later if some design in particular appeals to you."

The twins and Tommy sat on the floor nearby, gazes glued to the TV. Some super puppy show was on, and they were beyond absorbed. Guess we had all of that in front of us.

Jimmy carried in a large charcuterie board loaded up with crackers, fruit, meats, and cheeses. "Eat, people."

"Time to wash hands," said Lena, rising to her feet and corralling the children into a nearby bathroom. They went somewhat reluctantly.

"How about a karaoke room?" asked Mal.

"Not necessary." David plucked out a melody. "Hey, I think he just smiled."

"Probably gas."

"He likes the music," I said, craning my neck to see. "It does not surprise me at all that his first smile would be about his daddy and a guitar. My child has excellent taste."

"Four weeks is a little young, but who knows?" Jimmy sat on the floor on the other side of the baby.

"He didn't smile 'til I played Led Zeppelin." David smiled. "My son is a born rocker."

"You'll definitely need a library," said Anne. "A butler's pantry would be great too."

"And his and hers walk-in closets are a must," added Lena. "If we're making a list."

I shrugged. "A library and a butler's pantry would be cool. I don't know. It's a lot to decide. But we've been sharing a closet just fine for years."

"Guess David doesn't collect bespoke suits like Jimmy does," said Lena. "His tie collection alone takes up a cabinet."

"And they are all extremely useful and necessary." Jimmy flicked back his dark hair. The bangs were longer while the sides kept short. In keeping with him being the slick and smooth aspect of the band.

"Oh, absolutely," said his wife with a saucy wink.

"Are you two hinting at bedroom games?" asked Mal with a frown. "Gross, guys."

"Games?" Tommy selected a piece of cheese and shoved it in his mouth. And then attempted to say something that no one understood because his mouth was full of cheese.

"Eat first, son. Talk later," said Mal. "That's my boy."

The twins giggled.

"We figure we need a couple of indoor living areas so everyone can have their own space. An outdoor area, theater room, office, and after that we'll see," I said. "A pool, maybe. That would be nice in summer."

"How do you feel about a koi pond?" Mal loaded up a cracker before popping it into his mouth.

"Can't say I feel much about it at all," said David. "Hey. He did it again. Check it out."

Jimmy grinned at the baby. "That's something close to a smile, all right. A smirk, maybe?"

"It's probably because he heard my voice," said Mal, also talking with food in his mouth. Which answered the question regarding where Tommy had learned that trick. Then he started laying out some choice pieces of food on a small plate for his son.

"What a clever baby," I said, my heart getting that explosive, warm feeling again. It was in the way David's eyes were lit up. Both of my male folk were happy, and that was awesome. "Take a picture for me, please. If I move it might distract him and he'll stop."

Jimmy grabbed his cell out of his pocket and snapped off some shots. "Got it."

"Any progress with a name?" asked Lena, sitting back down.

"Actually, we have an announcement to make about that." I smiled.

David paused his fingers on the strings, and his son let out a cry of woe. "Guess I better keep playing."

"We were going to wait until everyone was together, but he's already a month old," I explained. "We can't keep calling him the baby forever. And I'm scared I'm going to mess up and give it away if we wait much longer. So, after much discussion and deliberations, we would like to present to you…"

David turned to me and smiled. "Jameson Malcolm Benjamin Ferris."

Anne's brows rose. "You're naming him after the whole band? I love it!"

"But his first name is Jameson, so he's got his own identity. It's just a little bit different." Lena clapped her hands. "It's such a great name."

I grinned outright. My heart was doing that warm full to bursting feeling again, and I couldn't be happier. This was it. This was our family. "We talked about it together long and hard. And the first time we came up with this particular combination, it just felt right. We both knew it. And the baby's little lips twitched which I'm certain means he was trying to smile."

"Jameson in honor of my big brother who's always looked out for me," said David, expression solemn. "And Malcolm Benjamin for my best two friends in the world."

"Plus I delivered the baby," added Mal. "Good work putting me before Benji."

"Jameson," said Jimmy. "Holy shit, guys. I'm honored."

"Sweared," mumbled Tommy, shoving some sliced ham into his mouth.

David smiled. "We've been calling him Jamesy. Just while he's little. He can make his own mind up about what he wants when he's older."

"It works," said Mal with a grin. "I like it. Excellent job."

"Welcome to the family, Jamesy." Lena sat back with a glass of wine in hand. "What a wonderful day."

* * * *

We were finally given the go-ahead to have sex six weeks after giving birth. Which meant it had been basically forever since we'd had any intimate relations. I don't think we'd ever gone this long over the course of our marriage. But what with David having been on tour previous to our baby boy's entrance into the world, it had been a while. You could forgive me for wanting to crack open a copy of *The Joy of Sex* to make sure I still knew how it was done.

Once Jude had left to do the groceries and Jameson was sleeping with the baby monitor turned on, David and I convened in the bedroom to discuss the matter. Like rational adults and not horn dogs. Because that would be undignified. We had the place to ourselves. Mostly. And there was no time to waste.

"What if it's different?" I asked, panting ever so slightly as he licked over my collarbone. Talk about goose flesh. From top to toe, I was one needy woman. Now if I could just get the few stray doubts out of my head. "Things might be weird down there. I don't know."

"Are you seriously doubting my love for your pussy?"

I laughed.

"You think I would judge or be harsh about the best vagina in the whole damn world?"

"I'm being serious."

"You're being silly," he said, moving up to nibble on my ear. My hot hands smoothed over his chest on account of him already being down to his boxer briefs and good God. My husband was beautiful. And I'd missed him so much. "There's never going to come a time when I don't want you, Evelyn. You're my girl. No matter how old we get or whatever. That is a definite."

"Thank you. And I'm keeping the ugly bra and breast pads on. Leaking milk mid-coitus is not cool."

"Okay." He kissed the mound of each breast. "Whatever you're comfortable with. You're not really worried about your body, are you?"

I winced. "Well, yeah…having a baby is kind of big."

"You're beautiful, baby. Trust me. I look at you and I can only see how wonderful you are."

"Thank you."

His gaze turned pained for a moment. "But we can stop and talk it through if you want. If that's what you need."

I looked down to where his hard-on tented the front of his underwear. "David. That was very sweet of you to offer considering the state you're in."

A grunt from him.

I slipped my hand down his boxers and wrapped firm fingers around his girth. His answering smile was magnificent. Beautiful inside and out, that was my man. Silken skin over hard flesh made my mouth water to taste. But there was no time for that, apparently.

"On the bed," he said, walking me backward. The haze of lust in his eyes was nothing less than thrilling. "Legs spread, baby."

"Huh." I pumped him once, twice. "Is that what you want?"

"You going to argue with me?"

"Hell no."

With a fiendish smile, he peeled down my panties then waited while I climbed onto the mattress. I couldn't catch my breath for some reason. Though the reason was kind of obvious, really. It had just been a while, and I was way overexcited.

David placed kisses on the arches of my feet, the insides of my knees, and on my slightly wobbly thighs. He licked his lips as he looked me over. Not missing a single thing. "No frowning," he said. "Every bit of you is beautiful."

I forced a smile.

He gave me a dour look before lowering his mouth to my cunt. The man did not mess around. Up through the lips of my labia he dragged the flat of his tongue. Oh. Wow. Yeah. Who even cared about cellulite? It was impossible to worry when my insides clenched and my whole body shivered with want. His strong hands held my legs wide open. And my husband knew me so well. How to make me sigh and catch my breath. Everything. Clearly he had no issues getting reacquainted with my lady parts. And with the attention he was paying them, he definitely held them in high esteem.

The tip of his tongue circled my clit before he suckled on my labia, making my blood run hot. His thumbs held me open as he French-kissed me down there. He licked me and loved me and ate me like a man starving. It didn't take long before pressure built down low. A knot between my hips tightened more with each passing moment. Then he sucked on my clit and whoa. I came with a gasp, eyes closed tight. Everything was white and sparkling and wonderful. My mind drifted somewhere up among the stars. I hadn't been this relaxed in a very long time.

And I'd wondered if I was too tired for sex. Ha. What a joke. Gimme.

"Baby, up you come." He carefully moved me farther up the bed, into the middle. There could be no waiting. Not only was David wanting, but the baby could wake up any minute. We'd definitely learned the value of getting things done during his nap times. Since I was back on birth control, which had better work this time, he crawled over me and wasted no time lining up the thick blunt head of his cock.

We both groaned as he slid home, the warmth of his body above me. My whole damn world right in that moment. I wrapped my legs around his hips and held back his hair with my hands. "God, I love you."

"Good," he said simply and started to move.

At first he was gentle, slow, and sweet. Which was nice, but it wasn't really us.

"David?"

He nuzzled the side of my neck. "Hmm?"

"Harder."

"Are you sure?"

"And faster." My smile was all teeth. "You're not going to break me."

"Whatever you want, baby."

As he pounded into me, his cock dragged back and forth over so many sensitive parts. It was like burning alive. How hot and real and raw we were. Sweat slicked our skin, and the scent of sex filled the air. We were all grasping hands and thrusting hips. Me rising to take him and him slamming home. If anyone walked away a little sore from our efforts, it really didn't matter. The only thing we cared about was reaching that high together.

One hand fisted my hair while the other slipped beneath my butt cheek, urging me on. Holding me close. Keeping me ready to take him again and again. And the whole time he stared into my eyes as if he could read me. Hell. I knew he could. Just like I knew him all the way. We were two halves of a whole and always would be. Our love had been tested, and we'd emerged victorious. Our lives had been irrevocably changed, and we were doing just great. Together.

His hips pistoned, and the tension in me grew higher and higher. He was strung taut like a wire, every muscle straining for release. The thick, hard length of him surged into me, filling all of the empty places. And the electricity surging up and down my spine dominated everything. I couldn't come again so soon. Surely not. But David wasn't taking no for an answer, and he knew my body so well. His hand slipped between us, skilled fingers teasing my clit. It was all too much, too beautiful. We were everything I'd ever need. The orgasm hit me with frightening intensity, my whole body seizing. Then the wave of pleasure rushed through me. With a feral snarl, David came too, hips bucking against me.

When I opened my eyes, he lay beside on the mattress. The bead of sweat on his shoulder called to me and why the heck not? I licked his skin. Salt and warmth and love. That's what he tasted like.

"Did you just lick me?" he asked, cracking open one eyelid.

"Yeah."

He laughed. "You're wild."

"No. We're wild."

All the love I'd ever need was in his gaze. "And thank fuck for that."

Epilogue

In the end, we chose to make our new home in a midcentury-modern house on the side of a hill with panoramic views. Like knock you on your ass it's so beautiful. It was a house of golden wood and gray stone with walls full of glass windows to let in the light. Unlike the house of sand that David had bought for his first girlfriend, however, it had a lovely simplicity. Or maybe it just didn't have the sordid heartbroken history that house had. This home had hope and a bright future. You could feel the good vibes as soon as you entered. And most importantly, there was room for us to grow. Not that I'd be volunteering for any more children anytime soon. No, thank you.

The house sat on plenty of land so we could add a guest house and a recording studio. Both of which were currently being built. Jude the excellent would be moving into the guest house as soon as it was finished. She'd become invaluable over the past six months. She took the antics of the baby, the occasional dash of crazy in our lives, and all of the rock stars in her stride. As for the recording studio, for David to be able to work from home would be awesome. And I think Lizzy was grateful everything wouldn't be happening at her and Ben's place all of the time. The guys could move around and give her a break. As much as we all loved each other, it was a lot to have the full band and entourage descending upon your house on the regular. It had already been decided that the next album would be recorded here.

And having all of our family here today made for a perfect housewarming. With the exception of the runaway baby situation.

"Jamesy, come back." I rushed after my crawling son. He could cross the rug in the main room at an alarming rate considering he'd only been crawling for a short while. Race car drivers had nothing on my child when he was determined to reach something. Putting security gates at the top of the staircase had been our first job when we moved. "Hey, buddy, slow down. You have a pants problem."

"I've got him," said Anne, bending over somewhat slowly on account of her pregnant belly. She was a brave woman going back for more. I still wasn't even sure what day of the week it was sometimes. Motherhood was hardcore. For a few weeks he'd decided to start the day at three a.m. That had seriously hurt. But we'd managed to get him back to a more livable routine.

I tickled his little feet. "I'm warning you, he needs a diaper change. I can smell it from here. It isn't going to be pretty."

"Poop doesn't scare me." Anne smooched the top of his head. "We'll clean you up in no time, my friend."

Jameson laughed in delight at all of the attention.

"Somebody smells," said David with a smile. "I can take him if you want."

"Ah," said Jameson. Which I think was short for Da, but he wasn't quite getting there yet. Whatever he was trying to say, it was adorable to hear him do it with such passion.

"Exactly. Ah. I was just about to say that myself. You are so clever. Now back off both of you. The baby is mine." Anne perched him on her hip and headed for the nursery.

Jameson stuck his thumb in his mouth and grinned. What a cutie.

Out by the heated pool, Ben was busy throwing small children into the water. Much to their very loud delight. The squeals and laughter echoed down the hill. Meanwhile Jimmy and Mal were in the deep end of the pool, ensuring everyone reached the side and climbed out safely. Lena and Lizzy were hanging out in the hot tub with mimosas. Sam and Martha were slow dancing on the deck. What with them both running their own businesses, they got damn busy. But they'd made the effort to be here with us today. In fact, everyone was here. Well…apart from my brother Nate and best friend Lauren, who had moved to Phoenix. And the protégé rock star Adam Dillon, who was on tour along with his partner Jill. Bon and Ziggy, our close security professionals, were up at the gate on account of some overly devoted fans hanging around. But we were never going to manage to keep our whereabouts a secret for long.

"How can I help?" David slung an arm around my shoulder, drawing me in for a kiss. Just a tease of his warm firm lips. Delicious.

"Everything is sorted. I'll set the food out in a little while and we can eat," I said. "Jude worked her ass off yesterday getting it all ready."

"She's a nice kid."

"A nice kid?" I raised my brows. "She's a grown woman."

"Yeah, I know." He smiled. "We should find someone decent for her."

I turned to stare at my love in wonder. "What is this? Are you turning into a matchmaker?"

"No."

"But yeah? Just a little?"

He shrugged. "She blushes bright red any time Jimmy's around."

"Oh really? I didn't know that." I tapped a finger against my chin. "So you want to distract her from her somewhat awkward crush by parading a little fresh man meat in front of her."

He frowned. "I wouldn't put it that way exactly."

"Of course not, you're way too smooth."

"I am." He laughed. "Thank you for noticing. It was Mal's idea, actually."

"Why does this not surprise me?"

"But Ben thought it was a good suggestion."

"You're all involved?" I asked. "Seriously?"

"It's not a big thing. It's just . . . a passing thought about helping out a valued friend and staff member."

"That you've all discussed. Poor sweet innocent single Jude. She isn't going to know what hit her."

"I may even already have someone in mind for her," he said. "A good guy. He's done well for himself over the last five years. And he's someone who'll be working with us on the new album."

"He'll just happen to be around, huh?"

"Yeah. Even Lena approved of my choice of potential boyfriends." He smiled. "Not that I'm going to make things weird or awkward. They'll just both be around. You never know what might happen."

"You really shouldn't interfere." I shook my head. "You know, of all the people I'd imagined might turn into hopeless romantics and try being Cupid, you were not on the list. Not even close."

"I just don't want her feeling uncomfortable and deciding to leave the position over my incredibly unattractive and very married brother. We like Jude, right?"

"We love her."

"That's what I thought. And Jameson adores her."

"It's all for the greater good, huh?" I smiled. "Oh, boy. Time for another Stage Dive adventure, I guess."

* * * *

Also from Kylie Scott and 1001 Dark Nights, discover Love Song, Closer, and Strong.

Sign up for the 1001 Dark Nights Newsletter
and be entered to win a Tiffany Key necklace.

There's a contest every month!

Go to www.1001DarkNights.com to subscribe.

**As a bonus, all subscribers can download
FIVE FREE exclusive books!**

Discover 1001 Dark Nights Collection Eight

DRAGON REVEALED by Donna Grant
A Dragon Kings Novella

CAPTURED IN INK by Carrie Ann Ryan
A Montgomery Ink: Boulder Novella

SECURING JANE by Susan Stoker
A SEAL of Protection: Legacy Series Novella

WILD WIND by Kristen Ashley
A Chaos Novella

DARE TO TEASE by Carly Phillips
A Dare Nation Novella

VAMPIRE by Rebecca Zanetti
A Dark Protectors/Rebels Novella

MAFIA KING by Rachel Van Dyken
A Mafia Royals Novella

THE GRAVEDIGGER'S SON by Darynda Jones
A Charley Davidson Novella

FINALE by Skye Warren
A North Security Novella

MEMORIES OF YOU by J. Kenner
A Stark Securities Novella

SLAYED BY DARKNESS by Alexandra Ivy
A Guardians of Eternity Novella

TREASURED by Lexi Blake
A Masters and Mercenaries Novella

THE DAREDEVIL by Dylan Allen
A Rivers Wilde Novella

BOND OF DESTINY by Larissa Ione
A Demonica Novella

THE CLOSE-UP by Kennedy Ryan
A Hollywood Renaissance Novella

MORE THAN POSSESS YOU by Shayla Black
A More Than Words Novella

HAUNTED HOUSE by Heather Graham
A Krewe of Hunters Novella

MAN FOR ME by Laurelin Paige
A Man In Charge Novella

THE RHYTHM METHOD by Kylie Scott
A Stage Dive Novella

JONAH BENNETT by Tijan
A Bennett Mafia Novella

CHANGE WITH ME by Kristen Proby
A With Me In Seattle Novella

THE DARKEST DESTINY by Gena Showalter
A Lords of the Underworld Novella

Also from Blue Box Press

THE LAST TIARA by M.J. Rose

THE CROWN OF GILDED BONES by Jennifer L. Armentrout
A Blood and Ash Novel

THE MISSING SISTER by Lucinda Riley

THE END OF FOREVER by Steve Berry and M.J. Rose
A Cassiopeia Vitt Adventure

THE STEAL by C. W. Gortner and M.J. Rose

CHASING SERENITY by Kristen Ashley
A River Rain Novel

A SHADOW IN THE EMBER by Jennifer L. Armentrout
A Flesh and Fire Novel

Discover More Kylie Scott

Love Song: A Stage Dive Novella

There's always the one that got away. Or kicked you out...

The new darling of rock 'n' roll, Adam Dillon, is ready to show his ex-girlfriend, Jill Schwartz, what a mistake she made kicking him to the curb. So maybe he wasn't the best of boyfriends. Writing great songs and climbing to the top of the charts isn't easy. Only problem is, he's fast finding out that success isn't everything.

* * * *

Closer: A Stage Dive Novella

When a stalker gets too close to plus-size model Mae Cooper, it's time to hire some muscle.

Enter former military man turned executive protection officer Ziggy Thayer. Having spent years guarding billionaires, royalty, and rock 'n' roll greats, he's seen it all. From lavish parties through to every kind of excess.

There's no reason some Instagram stylista should throw him off his game. Even if she does have the most dangerous curves he's ever seen...

* * * *

Strong: A Stage Dive Novella

When the girl of your dreams is kind of a nightmare.

As head of security to Stage Dive, one of the biggest rock bands in the world, Sam Knowles has plenty of experience dealing with trouble. But spoilt brat Martha Nicholson just might be the worst thing he's ever encountered. The beautiful troublemaker claims to have reformed, but Sam knows better than to think with what's in his pants. Unfortunately, it's not so easy to make his heart fall into line.

Martha's had her sights on the seriously built bodyguard for years. Quiet and conservative, he's not even remotely her type. So why the hell can't she get him out of her mind? There's more to her than the Louboutin wearing party-girl of previous years, however. Maybe it's time to let him in on that fact and deal with this thing between them.

An Excerpt from Strong: A Stage Dive Novella

"Martha," said Sam, raising his head off the edge to appraise my red bikini. "You look nice."

"Thank you." I set the glasses and bottle beside the tub. "Is this a set-up?"

"Not by me."

I frowned on account of it being my go-to expression.

"I'm out here every night after I finish my workout."

"Of course you are." I sighed. "Lizzy would know that."

For a moment he said nothing, his gaze fixed on my face as if he could read me. And he probably could. "Breeze is cool tonight, but the water's good and hot. Are you getting in?"

I nodded and carefully made my way down the steps into the as-promised beautifully warm bubbling water. It did feel dangerously good.

"What's in the bucket?" he asked.

I knelt on the step to inspect the bottle. "Fucking Cristal champagne. This is so a set-up."

"Doesn't say much if you have to be tricked into spending time with me," he said, tone deceptively light.

"You know that's not it."

"Do I? Because I can leave if you like."

With practiced ease, I popped the cork and filled the two glasses, handing him one. "Sam, will you please stay and have a drink with me?"

"Why, Martha, I'd love to." His big hand took the delicate glass from me. Everything about the man was solid, bulky. Not my usual type at all. Next to Sam, I felt positively delicate. Hilarious when you considered how many men I'd scared out of a second date. He made me wish I knew anatomy better. So I could put a name to all of the bumps and bulges in his shoulders and arms. His steamy wet shoulders and arms. "You're staring."

"Hmm?" I asked.

"You're staring at me. Sit down."

"Oh." I sat.

"No need to frown."

"I'm not frowning."

"Whatever you say." His voice was all placid and happy now. I amped my expression up to a scowl. An arm stretched across the edge of the tub, he put the glass to his lips, taking a sip. A wince. "Do you actually like this shit?"

"I don't mind it. Why, what do you drink?"

He took another sip, gaze thoughtful. "Red wine, beer, bourbon if I'm in the mood for liquor."

"The beer and bourbon make sense, but I'd never have picked you as a red wine aficionado."

"No? Nice to know I can still surprise you."

"Oh, you're all about the surprises lately."

About Kylie Scott

Kylie is a *New York Times*, *Wall Street Journal*, and *USA Today* best-selling, Audie Award winning author. She has sold over 2,000,000 books and was voted Australian Romance Writer of the year, 2013, 2014, 2018, & 2019, by the Australian Romance Reader's Association. Her books have been translated into fourteen different languages.

Discover 1001 Dark Nights

Ivy/Laura Wright ~ STRUNG UP by Lorelei James ~ MIDNIGHT UNTAMED by Lara Adrian ~ TRICKED by Rebecca Zanetti ~ DIRTY WICKED by Shayla Black ~ THE ONLY ONE by Lauren Blakely ~ SWEET SURRENDER by Liliana Hart

COLLECTION FOUR
ROCK CHICK REAWAKENING by Kristen Ashley ~ ADORING INK by Carrie Ann Ryan ~ SWEET RIVALRY by K. Bromberg ~ SHADE'S LADY by Joanna Wylde ~ RAZR by Larissa Ione ~ ARRANGED by Lexi Blake ~ TANGLED by Rebecca Zanetti ~ HOLD ME by J. Kenner ~ SOMEHOW, SOME WAY by Jennifer Probst ~ TOO CLOSE TO CALL by Tessa Bailey ~ HUNTED by Elisabeth Naughton ~ EYES ON YOU by Laura Kaye ~ BLADE by Alexandra Ivy/Laura Wright ~ DRAGON BURN by Donna Grant ~ TRIPPED OUT by Lorelei James ~ STUD FINDER by Lauren Blakely ~ MIDNIGHT UNLEASHED by Lara Adrian ~ HALLOW BE THE HAUNT by Heather Graham ~ DIRTY FILTHY FIX by Laurelin Paige ~ THE BED MATE by Kendall Ryan ~ NIGHT GAMES by CD Reiss ~ NO RESERVATIONS by Kristen Proby ~ DAWN OF SURRENDER by Liliana Hart

COLLECTION FIVE
BLAZE ERUPTING by Rebecca Zanetti ~ ROUGH RIDE by Kristen Ashley ~ HAWKYN by Larissa Ione ~ RIDE DIRTY by Laura Kaye ~ ROME'S CHANCE by Joanna Wylde ~ THE MARRIAGE ARRANGEMENT by Jennifer Probst ~ SURRENDER by Elisabeth Naughton ~ INKED NIGHTS by Carrie Ann Ryan ~ ENVY by Rachel Van Dyken ~ PROTECTED by Lexi Blake ~ THE PRINCE by Jennifer L. Armentrout ~ PLEASE ME by J. Kenner ~ WOUND TIGHT by Lorelei James ~ STRONG by Kylie Scott ~ DRAGON NIGHT by Donna Grant ~ TEMPTING BROOKE by Kristen Proby ~ HAUNTED BE THE HOLIDAYS by Heather Graham ~ CONTROL by K. Bromberg ~ HUNKY HEARTBREAKER by Kendall Ryan ~ THE DARKEST CAPTIVE by Gena Showalter

Kenner ~ FROM BLOOD AND ASH by Jennifer L. Armentrout ~ QUEEN MOVE by Kennedy Ryan ~ THE HOUSE OF LONG AGO by Steve Berry and M.J. Rose ~ THE BUTTERFLY ROOM by Lucinda Riley ~ A KINGDOM OF FLESH AND FIRE by Jennifer L. Armentrout

On Behalf of 1001 Dark Nights,

Liz Berry, M.J. Rose, and Jillian Stein would like to thank ~

Steve Berry
Doug Scofield
Benjamin Stein
Kim Guidroz
Social Butterfly PR
Ashley Wells
Asha Hossain
Chris Graham
Chelle Olson
Kasi Alexander
Jessica Johns
Dylan Stockton
Kate Boggs
Richard Blake
and Simon Lipskar

Made in the USA
Columbia, SC
07 November 2021